# AN OUTCAST LIFE

Ken Liljenquist

# AN OUTCAST LIFE

**TATE PUBLISHING**
AND ENTERPRISES, LLC

Published by Tate Publishing & Enterprises, LLC
127 E. Trade Center Terrace | Mustang, Oklahoma 73064 USA
1.888.361.9473 | www.tatepublishing.com

Tate Publishing is committed to excellence in the publishing industry. The company reflects the philosophy established by the founders, based on Psalm 68:11,
*"The Lord gave the word and great was the company of those who published it."*

Book design copyright © 2013 by Tate Publishing, LLC. All rights reserved.
*Cover design by Jan Sunday Quilaquil*
*Interior design by Jomel Pepito*

Published in the United States of America

ISBN: 978-1-62854-402-2
1. Fiction / General
2. Fiction / Family Life
13.07.24

1

*I am an artist that a mocking God*
*Condemns, alas! to paint the gloom itself.*

—Charles Baudelaire

I am eighteen years old, five and a half feet tall and just out of high school. I know people have tragedies in their lives and wonder, *Why me?* But this is different. My affliction is not concrete. I must be a target. I can't figure it any other way. From the time my family moved to Harden, I have been singled out. Kids from the school we moved from warned my older brother and sister that we were moving to a real bad town, but I didn't figure it could possibly affect me. I haven't the remotest idea why I have been chosen, but the attackers are real, and they are cold, dark shadows who creep up and hurl their pebbles, rocks, and boulders, hurting me in varied and intense ways.

Sometimes, I have seen them coming, but mostly, they have been lurking in the hidden places, waiting to be sure of a good, clean shot, and the pain they inflict is intense emotional, physical, and spiritual. I'm not speaking of a stinging type of pain that draws a flinch and leaves a small mark. These hurts are felt through my entire physical being and beyond to emotional frontiers with dark, lonely valleys and high, high towering cliffs, soaring bewilderingly past vision and imagination. They travel deep into an unknown sphere, feeding the roaring billows that fire and molten the spirit in me, forcing eruptions of rage, jealousy, anger, fear, hate, and love. Indistinguishable, they are the gray mass separating me from the world around me. That's why I am here in the vast open mountains, secluded and searching. *Who made me into a target? Why?* Hours upon hours have slowly filtered away while I have dug and chiseled through my dusty mind trying to strike that vein of knowledge keying my understanding and finding an escape.

I feel extremely uncomfortable around almost all people. All attention, good or bad, heats up my entangled emotions. My scalp tightens, and my hands begin to tremble. My neck and face sere with hot, prickly pain, and my jaw locks solid. Often, my eyes burn as small, warm masses gather to their corners. With one lightning dive, they hit my cheeks, cool quickly, and parade to my chin. There they hang conspicuously, like a child seeking attention, and, with an abrupt leap, mix into the fabric of my shirt.

I wonder what thoughts are being forged behind those cold, steely eyes that beam down at me. I would rather people pretend I'm not around and just ignore me. I do that very often. I close out the world and let my mind carry me to a green mountain meadow where a beaver so instinctively builds his world around him or a deer lovingly feeds its fawn. All the wildlife mingle, undisturbed among friends, not caring what's around because they have no need to fear anything.

The wind uses the tops of the trees as vanes, showing its freedom by blowing them in any direction it desires. No shadows can come here to hit me with their stones. I feel safe and at ease. But I have to live in that world. *That little town. How can such a small town cause too much pain? Why am I the target of that pain?* I have brothers, sisters, and maybe a few friends. And yes, they get hit occasionally like everyone else. But they don't have that constant pelting, wondering who and what attack will be next. *How severe or damaging will it be this time? Which tunnel or shaft will rail my load through this dark confusion to a shining hope?*

On the mountain peaks, I can separate myself from the rock throwers, but my emotions are still jagged sharp pathways upon which I can only painfully pursue any course hoping for an escape. Each venture through one crushing memory to another conveys me back to where I began: "Why?" The meteoric shower of attacks recently has forced my sudden retreat back to this, my fortress, more and more frequently. It is a long drive and a hard climb to sit and study this dense array of uniquely adorned granite mountains. From peaks to valleys, some round balding heads, covered with snow and graying shelves of rock, are weathered and hardened with age and laden with wisdom. These arouse my curiosity. *What lies beneath that aged exterior?* Others are adorned from their sharp peaks down through the smooth, spreading valleys with multiple shades of bright colors. Their blue-green pools dot the landscape, sending out sparkling messages of deceit and vanity. I know they are glossy covering over a harsh base of stone.

How very strange that even nature utilizes its own form of deceptive cosmetics to make appear beautiful what is ugly while leaving truth repressively bare and hideous.

To hike to these schools of learning is no less a wonder. To ascend quickly swells my legs with volcanic bursts of heat and searing pain. Hot and cold air gush through my gaping mouth, igniting a furnace within. Sweat, meant to cool me, stings my eyes and collects dust particles to itch and torment exposed skin. Brush and shrubs, barely visible to my occupied mind, flash welt raising sparks at a distinct target: me. In contrast, a slow nonchalant climb pacifies me into the ghostly pace of the undead. No pain, no confusion, no struggle to gain or progress. The cognizant shadows lie that pleasure is gain and gain is exploitive torment. But I know to reach the top means calm and rest. *Why am I eaten with confusion?* This arena of complications shows no hope for escape. Too many shadows sit in the stone bleachers, lusting for my suffering and anguish to intensify, but this is my fortress. I must come here to build and fortify against the conflict. I have to sort out that entity, me, and build walls that can withstand the constant assaults.

*So where did this all begin? Was my targeting chance selection, or was it by cruel design?* I work and dig deep into past memories to know what trail I have so painfully traveled. Perhaps a change of pathways will link me to that society from which I shrink. My thoughts, experiences, and deductions are from my point of view—a view perhaps distorted by uncommon circumstances. Still, I wonder why they have happened and what have they made of me. I try to fade back into my life to hear, see, and know my experiences. *Was there a beginning? Will there be an end?*

## 2

*Say to yourself at the start of each day, I shall meet with
meddling, ungrateful,
violent, treacherous, envious, and unsocial people. They
are subject
to all these defects because they have no knowledge of good
and bad.*

—Marcus Aurelius

"Oh, just ignore it!"

This was my Mom's answer to all problems. Though her answer didn't vary over the years, my reactions to it seemed to go through stages. The first time I heard it, confusion fogged my mind. *What sense is there to ignoring something that makes you cry, especially when it is a cruel personal attack?*

After the confusion stage came the stage of not wanting to accept it. I felt I had to figure things out.

Then there was the surprise stage. *How could "Just ignore it" be applied to a situation that requires some kind of action or response? As a child, there are situations that just seem to need adult intervention, so how do you just ignore it?*

The next stage was the anger stage. When situations came about which were so extremely important and I needed help only to get that "Just ignore it" crap, I would become infuriated.

After the anger came bitterness. Knowing that I was being wronged and that adults in particular knew it and seemingly didn't care made me very bitter. Certain situations were unfair and quite obviously so, yet I could not get redress.

Finally, I seemed to reach the acceptance stage. There was no justice to be found, so just accept it and walk away. "Just ignore it." Though I could accept this standard for myself, I couldn't bring myself to accept it as far as others were concerned. This was the cause of a few problems. I got into numerous fights because someone was, in my opinion, being unfairly treated.

*So how has this all contributed to what I am now?* Many circumstances and people are involved in everyone's lives, and perhaps we each see them differently. Maybe we all experience the same trials, but personalities absorb them and filter them in such varied ways as to spew out a final product that is much different than any other. But my experiences seemed much different than others around me. I didn't see my classmates being stoned so mercilessly and seeming to have no one sympathetic to their misery.

Going through the situations of Mom's "Just ignore it" philosophy wasn't so simple as to be confined to one circumstance in each stage. There was a slow evolution, which occurred over a period of years from childhood to young adulthood as those reactions that proved themselves without utility fell victim to the selective processes of trial and error. Possibly, these stages progress further, but at eighteen years of age, my experience dictates that if there is a wrong and you can't figure out a way to handle it, you must ignore it.

I reflect on one of my earliest recollections of hearing that phrase "Just ignore it." I don't recall my exact age, I guess three or four years old. We were driving at sunset, and the sky was glowing orange where the sun had just disappeared below the desert horizon. The stretching sands were a mass of strange shapes and shadows. At that early age, the sight was both a wonder and a fright. That brilliant orange color splashed across the broad sky began melting away in stages, darker and darker into a black horizon. Soon, gargoyle shapes were scattered abundantly across the desert flats. I wouldn't have wanted to get out of the car. Perhaps some of those shadows were alive. The worst part of the entire sight, though, was the fact that my hair was about as orange as the sunset. No sooner had the color orange been mentioned than Dad started in on my hair.

"Redhead, redhead, fire in the woodshed," he taunted.

That hurt my feelings deeply. *Why would my own Dad make fun of me?* It brought loneliness and shivers down my stomach through my chest. This was a feeling I would become well acquainted with. Then the other kids started in.

"He looks like a rooster with an orange comb."

"No, he looks like a carrot," someone else teased.

I asked them to be quiet, which only fueled their flickering fire. When I started to cry, Mom let me climb into the front seat next to her.

"Please make them stop, Mom," I begged between choking sobs.

"Oh, just ignore it," she said so nonchalantly.

*How bewildering. Just ignore that my Dad is encouraging my brothers and sisters to tease me and upset me?* I didn't know how to ignore it. The more they taunted, the more lonely I felt. I couldn't enjoy looking through the shadowing sands and the fading sunset. No, the still suspense of an evening, fascinating yet spooky, was washed away in a flood of confusion and tears. This was the beginning of the deforming of my emotions. One first step down a pathway, which ripped away emotional rationality, one which led me to hate, fear, and respect my father. Ironically, he forged and sealed those conflicting feelings from me toward him unknowingly, uncaring, or perhaps purposely.

At this very early age, the pattern was repeated often. Dad made the others tease me to a point of gross confusion. I hated it and would cry, and Mom would say to just ignore it. Often, the crying would last long and hard. My nostrils burned from tears tromping over the raw skin so frequently rubbed to keep my nose from running over my top lip. My head numbed and pounded on both sides. Eventually, I would feel as badly in my stomach. It would seem very empty, begin to churn, then tighten suddenly. These whirligigs of dizzying pain were paralyzing. I didn't want to move, cry, or think at all. Each of these would add to the terrible discomfort. I just wanted to sleep, fall away into a world of dark and quiet—no pain, no tormentors from within or without, no more confusion for a while.

Sometimes when I would wake up, I'd have an awful pounding headache. Every tiny movement—walking, breathing, thinking—drove lightning bolts of pain up both sides of my scalp and through my skull. At these times, I tried to find a cool, soft hideaway, a basement chair or a green, shaded retreat. It evolved into a routine that would help but not always—close my eyes; relax my mind, my head, my neck; let my shoulders droop and loosen. A magical door would open, and the gruesome pain scamper tauntingly away into the air. Such a wonderful relief. At times, I would awaken without a headache and feel fresh and alive as after a cleansing rain. I wanted to get out and run and play, burn up some wild energy.

But at the end of the day, I had still been taught to fear my Dad. *What kind of pain would result from his presence alone? When would his mood open the shadowy doors in his mind release those imps to throw those barbed insults at me?* Over the years, the fear intensified as I always looked for some hint of apology, a signal that he cared even a little. But no signal, not the slightest display of love or acceptance ever came, only those shadows waiting for the mood so I could be his target.

At times I could see the imps in his eyes, dancing and mocking, laughing and warning, "Soon our fun will begin. You can count on it." *Would he ever turn against them and be my friend, my ally, a father?* No, it never has happened even up to now. We have become enemies, but for what hidden reason? I'm not even sure that his attacks are consciously arranged. There just seems to be some dark feelings overshadowing our relationship.

*How do you live with a person for eighteen years and never have any kind of constructive conversation? How can you not get to know them, at least a little bit, in that length of time?* The harder I have knocked at those closed, wooden doors of his mysterious heart, the harder I have been knocked down. *Is it worth all the pain to try to gain entrance into what appears to be such a dark and hateful world?*

I believe that a time comes with some challenges, which require one to acknowledge the inability to conquer and to walk away and ignore the lost time and effort, no matter what the cost has been. At such a time, the reward is the learning gained through the experience. If carefully digested, it can prove to be a valuable deterrent in preventing personal tragedies.

# 3

*In taking revenge, a man is but*
*even with his*
*enemy; but in passing it over,*
*he is superior.*

—Francis Bacon

I was in the second grade when I reached the second response stage to Mom's "ignore it" philosophy. My brother and I were separated by barely a year in age. Most things I did with others, he was there. Some unspoken, unrealized bond kept him almost always around me. If I wasn't with him, I was usually alone. While he played with his friends at school, I stood at a distance and watched. He was confident and aggressive in all his actions. He seemed to me to be at peace within himself. I was always apprehensive, sensing something wrong. I would watch and make certain he wasn't a target. I knew the feelings, and I hated them. I couldn't allow him to be mistreated, except by myself or my parents.

One afternoon, we were out relaxing on the front steps of our home. Our house was comfortable and had plenty of room for us six kids. My brother and I were plotting our daily activities. We were talking when we saw a pack of dogs coming down the road—the perfect target for dirt clods. We loved to throw at anything: animals, bottles, cans, old cars, sticks in the canal, and even each other. Today it would be dogs. We ran to the edge of the lawn where dirt separated our yard from the road. The road grater came by often enough to keep us plentifully supplied with clods to throw.

We quickly filled our hands so full that the crowding smashed much of our ammo. We attacked and just a few throws left us with no targets. My brother had run up the road for an extra shot or two and was now where the dogs had been.

A neighbor boy lounging in his yard was watching us.

I threw a clod that exploded into small pieces on my brother's shoulder. He came charging at me with a fresh handful. I was empty and ducked frantically to avoid being hit. I couldn't look away from him to pick up more ammo or he would surely hit me, so I grabbed blindly for a clod and threw it quickly. His supply was depleted so he turned to retreat. My shot nailed him squarely in the back. The clod, it turned out, was a rock, and it dropped him screaming in pain. I knew he would cry for a while and then let it go because it was an accident. We had plenty of those while we were growing up.

I started to run to help him and felt a sharp pain on the left side of my back. Air burst from my lungs, and I fell to my knees. I gasped for air but couldn't breathe. My head was thundering with pain and blackness except for the flashing lights darting in every direction. I became dizzy and nauseous. My arms were limp and helpless, and I fell face first into the dirt. My neighbor skipped by laughing.

"How does it feel getting the same thing you gave your brother?"

I heard my brother holler and chase him to his trailer across the street from our home. Then he came back and helped me inside to the couch. I could breathe and move my arms and legs, but my back was screaming with pain. My head ached, and stars were still circling. I blubbed out the story to Mom. I was sure she'd see that the jerk was punished. My cheeks were soiled with teary mud, and there were small grains of dirt on my lips and in my mouth.

"Oh, just ignore it," she calmly passed it off. "He didn't mean anything by it."

*Ignore this horrid pain?* The horror of the inability to get air into my lungs was terrifying. She was indifferently telling me to ignore that this kid had purposely tried to kill me! *What sense does that make?* I hadn't imagined such pain even existed. *How on earth was I to ignore it?* And the kid walked away laughing. His laugh still echoed through my throbbing mind. To ignore it wasn't the proper solution.

A couple hours later, I was able to get up and move. My head still hurt. I looked out the window and saw the neighbor heading past our house. I knew he was going to the store for candy. That's what all the kids in the neighborhood were doing when headed in that direction. I went out to where I had been when I was hit. There was a huge dirt clod, dried and hard as a rock. It wouldn't have broken even if I had thrown it onto the pavement. I took the clod and hid. If he saw me, I wouldn't get as good a shot as I wanted. I knew it was necessary for him to learn a lesson about hurting other people, especially me. No one could know that kind of pain without experiencing it for themselves. To let him learn from personal experience surely made more sense than to just ignore it.

As he neared, I became over anxious and almost blew it. Just as he turned to run, I heaved the clod with all my might. I heard a dull thud. The clod rammed into his neck just below the ear. Bewildered, he turned to face me. His expression was that of shock. His face flashed a weird green color, then slowly dissolved to a very white pale, and his lips turned purple. I wondered if he felt as badly as I had. Then he screamed an awful gurgling groan, which raised goose bumps across my skin. I knew that wasn't just from the surprise of the attack. Those colors, that look of absolute hurt in his eyes, and that groaning scream which was choked off by the tightening of his body meant that he had felt real pain. He surely had learned his lesson.

I had no fear of punishment because I knew I had taken the proper action.

When I turned to go to the house, I realized a tingling sensation and a soreness in my wrist form the throw.

I never developed any outside friendships. I assume it was because my family moved often. It took me a long time to make friends. My brothers and sisters always had them. This left me out because they often got to go places and do things with their friends' families, important places like carnivals and rodeos, which my father never took us to. I had lots of time alone, so I daydreamed often for hours at a time. I mostly dreamed about being a super athlete. Once in a while, this would get me into trouble.

A time in particular occurred while we were living in a small town prior to moving to Harden. We had a very large and wide driveway covered with loose rock. One day, three of my brothers and I built small forts in the driveway to hide behind and have rock fights. When someone got hit, they would cry for a while, and then we'd get back to fighting. One day after Mom called us for dinner, I stayed in my fort, dreaming. I was caught up in being a great track star and performing a major upset in the Olympics to win a gold medal.

One of my brothers hollered for me to come eat. I put my hand on the top edge of the fort to lift myself up. It was a wall about three feet high and six feet long made of half-inch plywood. Just as my hand wrapped over the edge of the plywood, I was gripped with a burning pain in my fingers. I heard a crunching sound, and my fingers began to throb violently. I screamed in agony, and my body chilled. The backs of the middle and ring fingers were soaked in blood, and loose skin hung around the edges of the wounds. I was too sick to look up or move. My stomach churned mercilessly. I heard my youngest brother laughing.

"You thought you were fooling me hiding there, didn't you?" he giggled.

I looked toward him and he threw a rock he was holding, barely missing my head. I weakly crawled to the house and entered, dripping blood and tears. I cried to my Mom.

"He was just playing," was her reply. "Just ignore it, and the pain will go away.

It hurt a long time, and I couldn't ignore it until the pain did go away. I wondered what kind of crisis it would take for Mom not to ignore it.

Up to this time, the teasing and the major physical hurts were the only real pain that I had experienced. But the shadows were about to leap into my life and follow and haut me continually even to the present time.

4

*At the grade school and high school levels…there's*
*definitely*
*been more violence, more drugs and*
*more dropouts.*

—Ron Paul

It was midway through my fifth grade year we moved to Harden. Many kids had told my older brother and sister that Harden was an awful place, what they called a hoodlum town—kids fighting, drinking, smoking, drugs, teen pregnancies, and the works. All the gross sins that we were drilled against during that time in our lives were part of that town. I didn't think much about it though. I had no reason to believe anyone in that town would bother me. I could just mind my own business like I always did. I was enough of a loner that I wouldn't attract attention.

My first day at school in Harden set the course for the following seven plus years. I should never have set foot in that school or even that town.

I never had liked attention at all, so when the teacher introduced me to the class, I blushed uncomfortably, and my insides quivered. Luckily, she wasn't much on introductions.

"Class, we have a new student." As she introduced me, her tone was stiff and abrupt.

"You sit in that seat," she ordered pointing to a desk two rows from the middle of the room.

I hurried to my seat thankful to get the attention away from me. My entire body was shaking and tingling with an unusual case of nervousness. I felt like stares were boring into the back of my head and neck. I carefully reached my hand back and stroked from the crown down. It wiped away some of the uncomfortable feeling, so I repeated it, rubbing harder.

We were given some math to do, and the teacher sat down. I liked math and finished quickly, then cautiously looked over my new class. I didn't want the teacher seeing me gazing around, so I could only look to the sides. Kids were quiet and seemingly studying hard.

I looked at the teacher. She was a short, moderately hefty woman. By her appearance, she was probably strong and no one to tolerate disrespect. She had a stony expression that reminded me of a prison warden. One glare from that stern face would be as effective as pointing a weapon at someone.

*Boy, are all the teachers here that way?* I wondered.

I thought of the appearance of the building as I had come in earlier. It was tall, six floors, old, faded yellow brick, with hard, gray, concrete steps leading into the building and up each floor.

The class was coldly quiet. I got chills as I listened and wondered if this was really a detention cell. I started looking at some of the students. So many plain and expressionless faces. I was suddenly overwhelmed with homesickness for my old school. I had had an older teacher who smiled often. We played games in her class and took special time to go outside for various activities. I was sure there would be none of that here. My stomach began to ache, and I became aware of sweat running down my sides. My shirt was loose and baggy and hanging away from my body allowing the small beads to run almost to my waist before being absorbed into the fabric. I wiped away the blanket of wetness, which now covered my forehead.

"Are you through with your work?" screeched the teacher.

I looked up and my jaw and cheeks tightened with fear. She was staring directly at me. I opened my mouth and squeaked but couldn't speak. I knew she expected a quick answer, so I nodded my head yes. Her eyes squinted and an already threatening face turned to a frown as she started toward me.

"Let me see," she demanded.

I was sure I had done them right. They were too easy. I wondered why everyone else was still working. Suddenly, I was hit with a bomb of panic. *What if they have a different kind of math here? What if I had done all of these wrong?* She looked at my paper with split-second glance and walked away. My face was on fire. I could feel more of those dark eyes from all directions. I quickly shot a glance to my left. A girl was staring at me with the same facial expression as the teacher. *They must all be that way*, I worried. I stared down at my desk lonelier than I had ever been before.

"Oh well, I wasn't here to make friends anyway," I tried to comfort myself.

I wondered what it was. The day had already dragged longer than any other in my lifetime. Perhaps I should go tell the teacher I was sick and needed to go home. No, I wouldn't dare. There was no telling how this lady would react to that. Besides, even if I went home, Mom might just send me back. That kind of attention I surely didn't need.

The teacher scooted her chair back noisily and got up to leave the room. I guessed she was just tempting anyone to dare make a noise in her class. She probably had a hidden tape recorder to catch the kids being rowdy so she could punish them. There were no sighs of relief as she left. The tension in the room was still thick.

A quick glance showed that all were still at work. *How could such easy math take them so long? What if it wasn't long? There was no clock in the room. What if time in this place was just slower than my other school?* I was trapped, scared, and isolated in a room full of total strangers. I longed for freedom.

"Ouch," I involuntarily blurted.

There was a sharp sting on my neck. A rubber band lit on the floor nearby. I picked it up and looked behind me. There was another girl who looked like the teacher. I peered into her eyes, and there were those same impish shadows I could always see in Dad's eyes. Trouble must be brewing. Just behind her sat a boy with slicked back, dark red hair. For a boy, he had very good features. I figured he was popular, especially with the girls.

"That's my rubber band. Give it back," he jeered.

I broke it and handed it back to him. The girl next to me grabbed my pencil and threw it to him. He laughed as he broke it.

"I'll see you at recess," he challenged.

The teacher reentered the room, and all was quiet again. The sweat which had heated me earlier was now a mat of cold dew tormenting my chattering bones. I wanted to leave there and never come back. I didn't want to fight. I was sure this whole group would step in and tromp me. Maybe I should tell the teacher. I looked at her. No way. Now I really was sick. I needed to go home but knew I would have just as cold a reception there as I was having here.

When the bell rang, the girl behind me tapped me on the shoulder.

"It's sure gonna be fun watching you get your butt kicked."

I stayed in my seat. After everyone was gone, the teacher looked up.

"Go to recess," she ordered.

I knew I had no choice. Our class was on the fifth floor, so I took my time going down the stairs hoping the bell might ring before I got outside. At the first floor, another teacher ordered me outside. No one was allowed inside during recess. I walked slowly out the door, and chants and yells began. Not only did everyone know I was had, but they were excited to see it happen. *Why would they all be so against me?* I didn't even know these people. In our old school when someone new moved in, it was exciting and fun. Everybody wanted to get to know them and where they had come from. I had never seen nor heard of any fights at that school. *What kind of hell was this?*

I was quickly surrounded by a mob of screaming kids and forced to the rear of the building. I prayed the commotion would bring a teacher. I became very frightened and weak. Even if I wanted to fight, I didn't have the strength. My hands, arms, and upper body began to shake uncontrollably, and I was breathing hard and fast. A small opening formed, and my opponent stepped out of the crowd of fanatical boys and girls. And of course, right there in front of the group stood that girl with the black shadows in her eyes. Everyone was laughing and taunting. I felt a stinging jolt on my cheek. Then another on my forehead. I tensed up and started to cry. *How could all these kids hate me?* They didn't even know me. Warm streams of tears were flowing down my face. The hits hadn't really hurt enough to worry about, but the feelings inside me were hurting profusely. I was flooded with a sense of worthlessness. I thought I could probably fight back and really hurt this kid, but I had no desire for that. I was too upset and too lonely to care about hurting someone else. I was stunned that in this whole crowd not one person would side with me. Shame filled my soul while I cowered like a frightened pup. I'd never had high opinions of myself before. But these feelings stamped a permanent brand into the recesses of my mind—that I was a cry baby and a weakling.

A commotion to one side drew attention briefly away from the fight.

"Grab that kid. He's the dork's brother," someone yelled.

I looked over to see a big, fat kid with freckles and hair as bright red as mine. *Grab my younger brother?*

"Fight back. You know you can whip that bum," he hollered at me. "Let go of me, and I'll fight your tough buddy," he sneered at the fat boy.

Another boy grabbed my opponent's arm and told him to just drop it. This boy had black hair and a dark complexion and was quite a good-looking kid. When he spoke, I could tell the group all respected him.

"Ya, let's go," the impish-eyed girl said. "He's nothing but a big crybaby, has to have his younger brother fight his battles."

"Why didn't you kill him?" my younger brother demanded of me. "You know you could have whipped him."

"I didn't want to fight with all those kids around. And you don't need to be butting into my problems."

I didn't even want him around me right then. I wished I could just disappear and never exist again. Walking back to class, I kept my head down and hurried to my seat. Now I felt more ashamed than ever. I wasn't afraid of that boy. I was afraid of fighting. It wasn't sore at all where he had hit me. For certain, I could have earned some respect if I had fought back. But when I thought of hitting someone with my fists, I cringed. I knew it wasn't right.

5

*It is proper to learn even from an enemy.*

—Ovid

I didn't tell anyone at home about the incident, and my brother promised not to either. It would blow over, and I would be fine.

For the next couple of weeks, I spoke to no one at school, and no one spoke to me. I might as well have been a ghost; it was like I didn't even exist. Nothing good happened. Nothing really bad, either: no looks, or comments. The other kids didn't acknowledge my presence in any way. I walked around in a strange void. At recess, I just stood under a big, old cottonwood tree. When the cold wind blew, the wide friendly body of the tree protected me. The chattering of its leaves echoed comforting sounds to my aching mind. I stood and watched the other kids play, laugh, and chase one another. I was glad I didn't have to worry about their attention.

We had to eat hot lunch at school unless we had a note from home and showed our lunch to our teacher. It was about a two-hundred-yard walk across the playground to the school where the lunchroom was located. There was one narrow flight of dull concrete steps down to the basement lunchroom. The door was heavy and hard to open, then echoed as it banged shut. The single, little room was always crowded and sounded like a busy hive of swarming bees. It was closed-in and dingy, the lighting dull, and, overall, the place was more like prison than the rest of the school. The food was usually worth going for though. I loved mashed potatoes and gravy with green beans, which were served there frequently. This and going home were the only parts of each day that I looked forward to.

One noon hour while walking back to our school, I was eating a cookie that I had brought from lunch. Suddenly, my hips shot forward, and my neck snapped back hard.

"You stinkin' piece of chicken crap," someone yelled.

I looked behind me to see a foot still cocked for a second blow, and a face I wasn't familiar with. My cookie had broken, and most of it was scattered on the ground. Another boy picked up the pieces of the cookie and demanded that I eat them, mud and all. I just started walking away. The kicker grabbed my arm and threatened to punch me if I didn't fight him.

"Come on," he scowled. "You either fight or cry, crybaby."

I looked the two of them over. I was small for my age, and these two were both smaller than I was. The kicker had slick, greasy, black hair, and pants pegged so tight I was surprised he could lift his leg to kick without splitting them. His shoes were black, pointed toe with a high gloss shine. It was obvious that appearance meant a lot to him. The other boy looked like a poor imitation of the first—not enough grease to keep his hair perfect, scuffs on already dull shoes, and clothes not as fresh and wrinkle free. I noticed a couple places in the leg seemed on his pants where they had started to come unpegged. I didn't care how popular dress like that was, I couldn't feel comfortable in such a clown suit.

"Are these friends of yours?" a voice interrupted my thoughts.

The two troublemakers jumped nervously at the sound. My older brother had come out of the junior high that was between my school and the lunch room. They panicked and took off running.

"What was going on here?" he asked.

"Oh, nothin', I think they thought I was somebody else."

I hadn't seen the two boys before, so I was surprised when I went into class and the scruffy one was in the back of the room. He must have been at the gathering my first day of school.

For the rest of the week, I ate quickly and hurried back to class. The two boys tried to cause trouble on occasion but were always scared away by one thing or another. They acted nervous and never said nor did anything while others were around. They just tried to sneak up and catch me alone. They reminded me of watching magpies trying to eat a road kill but always being chased off by oncoming traffic.

On Monday, while eating lunch, I saw them come into the lunchroom. Before getting their food, the slick one came over and told me I'd better wait outside for him or else. I almost started laughing as I thought, *This kid isn't just small. He is extremely stupid. Could he really think anyone could go out and wait for him to come bother them?*

I ate quickly and hurried back to school. The following day, they didn't even come into the lunchroom. I was surprised but relieved. I sat and enjoyed my meal. They must have finally wised up. When I left, they were at the bottom of the stairs. The slick one grabbed and pushed me up against the door. Swearing, he said, "I told you to wait yesterday. Why didn't you do it?"

His grip on me was laughably weak. I began to wonder what kind of home he came from. It surely must be a troubled one. This must all be some absurd extension of that. I jerked my shoulder free to leave, and he hit me in the eye. I walked away and kept going. My eye was stinging and full of tears, not because I was crying, but because he must've gotten his knuckle into it. He and his buddy swore after me, laughing and congratulating each other on their successful crusade. I didn't think they would bother me anymore, now that they had gotten a perverse thrill from hurting me.

Wednesday, I went to the lunchroom and again ate quickly. I didn't look around. I just got up and left. Halfway back to school,

I heard the two tormentors coming. They ran up, and one grabbed my arms while the other punched me in the stomach. I started to fight my way loose, and it was too easy. I looked behind me and saw slicky on the ground. My younger brother had seen them and hurried over to help me. The kid got up, and my brother told him we were going to kick their behinds.

"Sure, your brother is nothin' but a chicken. He'll probably stand there and watch us beat you up," the scruffy one mused.

"He could whip both of you if he wanted to," my brother bragged. "He just doesn't like to fight. If you bother him again, we are going to beat the heck out of both of you."

Slicky looked at me. "How's it feel to have your baby brother stick up for you, you sissy?"

"Tomorrow you wait so I can go to lunch with you," my brother suggested when the two attackers had stalked off.

I didn't wait, but he got there while I was still eating.

"I told you to wait for me," he complained.

"They're not going to bother me anymore," I replied. "They are afraid now that someone else is involved in it."

When we left the lunchroom, they were both there, and they had the fat kid who had held my brother at the fight my first day of school. There was also another boy whom I didn't recognize. The fat one started for my brother, and I instinctively raised my fists and jumped between them.

"If you want to fight that badly, then I will fight you. I will fight each one of you separately."

I felt no fear at all. I couldn't and wouldn't let them pick on my brother. I was boosted by a surge of anger and hatred swept away the fear I had known previously. I needed to protect him from the feelings I was forced to experience. I figured that now by fighting them, I could put an end to all this garbage.

My reaction caught them off guard. They all backed away and threatened to get us the next day with more help. That evening, I told Mom what had been going on. I knew it was time to get some adult intervention before this got out of hand. I was afraid my brother might get hurt seriously. He had a short temper and would try and take on a whole gang if they showed up.

"Oh, just ignore it," Mom scolded. "Why don't you learn to stay out of trouble? Besides, they're just being boys. By tomorrow, they will have forgotten all about it."

I tried to make Mom understand, but I soon realized she didn't want to get involved in it. I knew this situation wouldn't just go away and probably wouldn't end without some adult intervention. This and the fact that she was my mother and should care about what was happening made me wonder if she gave a hoot about me at all.

Friday, I skipped lunch. That was the only way I could see to ignore this situation. When I got home, I was starving.

"Didn't you eat lunch at school today?" Mom demanded.

"No, I didn't want to get beat up. If I go to the lunchroom, a group of boys will gang up on me."

"Well, from now on, I'll give you a beating if you don't eat at school," she promised.

My lunch ticket had run out, so on Monday, I just kept my lunch money and went to the drugstore to eat. I bought a root beer float. After that, some days I'd go there, some to the store, and others to the drive-in by the high school. I never could get to eat very much because a week's worth of money for school lunch didn't buy much anywhere else. It was great though. My lunches were yummy now, and no one bothered me. I got away with this for a few weeks.

When Mom gave me my lunch money one Monday, I went to the store and bought a bag of candy bars. I figured by not going uptown so often, there was less chance of getting caught. I decided to eat one or two candy bars each day.

On Tuesday, our teacher said anyone not eating in the lunchroom was to stay in class with their lunch. I wasn't worried because I just wouldn't eat till she was gone. Only two of us stayed. The other was a girl who had her lunch out quickly and was eating.

"Are you eating cold lunch?" the teacher asked me.

"Yes," I replied.

"Then let me see it."

Something in the way she said that made me nervous. That stone-cold face had a little color in it. I could see some hint of evil pleasure in her eyes. Maybe someone told on me. Her rock hard voice varied in pitch a little as if to imply a slight friendship or kindness. I began to open my desk very slowly. I kind of looked at her as though I'd lost it.

"Well, do you have a cold lunch or not?" she asked a little too patiently.

Realizing her tone was a tiny bit friendly gave me courage. I could explain it to her and she'd understand. I pulled the candy out, which was still in a brown paper bag. She wanted to see inside. I pulled out the candy bars and gave her a weak smile, thinking she might see some humor in it all.

"I thought so," she boomed.

No nice tone now. She sounded like a wicked witch. She started toward me, and I braced myself for a hard blow. Instead, she clamped a steel grip on my arm and practically lifted me and the desk off the floor as she demanded that I go with her. I was terrified and looked over at the girl. I guess I must have hoped she could somehow help. Maybe if she said we were sharing lunch, I'd be set free.

I was marched or I suppose I was actually dragged to the principal's office. It was in the same building as the lunchroom. Many kids saw the teacher hauling me along and were gasping as we passed by. I was sure this warden and the principal were going to beat me mercilessly. From the experiences I had already had with the kids here, I figured these two would probably gang up on me and work me over before they called my Mom. I became very sick to my stomach. I tried to stiffen my legs to slow our speed but was just dragged effortlessly along by my captor. My arm was beginning to throb from her iron-tight grip. It started cramping, and my fingers and hand were going numb. I felt so guilty and ashamed. I tried to reason away the guilt on the grounds that I was completely innocent of any wrongdoing. Nevertheless, I couldn't overcome the awful feelings. I wanted to cry, but no tears would come. I thought how nice it would be if Mom would be there at the principal's office to tell them to just ignore it.

The principal was an older woman. She was thinner than my teacher but with just as stony an expression. Her face was long compared to the round one my teacher had. She looked weathered and reminded me of the older farm ladies at church. In fact, as I studied her, I realized we went to the same church. She even had a son my age. Maybe she wouldn't hurt me after all.

"Why have you been skipping lunch?"

Her voice was more pleasant than the teacher's but still demanding.

My neck was aching. The teacher had let go of my arm, but it still hurt and so did my shoulder. My head and face were tight. I was already getting a headache. I tried to answer, but my mouth sealed. My lips were sucked together. I tried to speak with my eyes, but she couldn't understand. I was petrified.

"All right then, we'll just call your mother and see what she has to say about this," the principal said.

I was very lightheaded by this time and hot. I was sweating and trembling. Dizziness swirled through my mind and lightning flashes bolted endlessly throughout my skull and in front of my eyes. I longed to just go home and relax in a shelter away from the world.

Since Mom already knew what had been going on, she would be sympathetic and maybe even explain it to the principal. This thought gave me a ray of hope.

We only had one car, and Dad had it at work so Mom couldn't come pick me up. The principal took me home. Her car was the nicest I had ever ridden in. The seats were clean and new-looking with no marks or tears.

With the large family we had, we didn't buy new cars, and all the activity in the car usually left tears and marks on all the seats.

Mom was waiting at the front door for us. She was pleasant with the principal while being told of my behavior. It seemed odd to me that Mom didn't mention the things I had told her about. I knew that any kid who got in trouble with these teachers and principal wouldn't want to cause trouble again. If Mom would be on my side, those kids would get what they deserved.

Finally, Mom said good-bye without giving any explanation for my behavior. She thanked the principal and came into the kitchen where I was waiting.

"You damned piece of crap," she screamed at me.

Before I could react, she had picked me up by my hair. My scalp burned where the hair was stretched to the limit. I was sure the whole patch would pull loose, skin and all. After shaking me awhile, she threw me down and attacked with full force. She slapped me viciously on the head, ears, and face.

My lips were quivering, and tears blurred my vision. An annoying hum vibrated in my ears. A sharp pain in my neck made me jerk away from her instinctively.

"Don't you jerk away from me," she screamed as she assaulted me again.

I became numb to the blows, but it all tore at my emotions. I had no defense. I was guilty of some horrible crime of which I couldn't comprehend. Her blows were echoing through my head. I couldn't speak or move. I just had to wait until she was finished. It lasted eternally. Even when she finally stopped, I still felt the blows and a horrible ringing in my ears. I looked up at her, and her face was streaked with red, white, and purple hatred. Her eyes were wide and still threatening, so I didn't dare to even breathe. I was sure the smallest movement would ignite another storm.

As our eyes met, she grabbed a handful of hair and began shaking it violently again. I was experienced in the physical pain of it all, but the confusion of my emotions overwhelmed me. I hurt so badly inside that I began to cry uncontrollably. My heart pounded against my chest. It would lunge hard then come to a dead stop only to lunge again and sink quietly back. I was sure my life was near to an end, either from Mom's beating or from my heart exploding.

Questions began to scream through my mind. *Why was I different than other kids? What was it that even made adults hate me so viciously? Why did my own Mom want to work so desperately hard to hurt me?* I was struck with a realization that she didn't care what had been happening to me at school. All she cared about was being forced to go against her ignore it philosophy. She was cornered into being involved, and that made her fight. *But why fight against me when she knew I was in the right?*

When she turned her back, I hurried downstairs to my bed. I wasn't long in confusion before I blanked out the world, and the blackness closed around me.

6

*What art thou that usurp'st this*
*time of night.*

—William Shakespeare

Being hauled to the principal's office the way I had been and
being kicked out of school for the day scared away my tormentors
for the rest of that school year. Kids not only ignored me but
acted like I was a plague. This was welcome treatment compared
to what I had gone through previously.

My summers were truly vacations. With brothers and sisters, I
spent most of my time swimming, fishing, hunting, and camping.
We weren't around our parents very often. Dad was too busy
earning a living for a large family, and Mom was just as busy
keeping up with cleaning, laundry, and a big garden to help feed
us all. Even when we were camping, Dad used that time to get
away from us, and Mom watched the little kids. The rest of us ran
wild through the hills and fished with one another. Dad loved to
fish and wouldn't tolerate any interference, so we seldom saw him.

Sometimes we would visit relatives or they us. We children
were not often allowed to speak to the adults and usually not
permitted to go into their houses. I didn't mind this except that I
wanted to know my grandparents. At the age of eighteen, I only
have my two grandmothers living, and I hardly know them. My
Dad's Dad died when my Dad was about seventeen. My Mom's

Dad died when I was in the third grade. I don't think Dad's Mom ever visited our home. When we visited her, which was very seldom, we were never allowed into her home, not of her will but of Mom and Dad's. It wasn't a big deal while we were younger because there was a large park nearby where we loved to play.

As much as I loved my summer vacations and as bad as school was, for some weird reason I always looked forward to the start of each new school year. Maybe I believed each year would be better than the last.

The sixth grade didn't justify that hope. I wasn't new any longer and expected to be a little more accepted than I had been the previous year. Right from the beginning, I was treated the same as where I had left off. I was some kind of leper socially. The boys wouldn't invite me to play in their recess games, so I tried to keep to myself and just daydream. On the playground, I always felt like the lone Christian in the stone arena. All those cold, hard eyes were watching me, waiting to see what would be my fate.

The boys would choose teams and play keep-away with a football. One team member would get the ball and toss it to his teammates to see how long they could keep it from the other team. When the ball was loose on the ground, everyone would kick, dive, pull, and whatever else to gain control of it.

Since I was never picked to be on a team, I would mostly run around hard and fast to just run out my frustration and loneliness. I ran until my lungs burned with the pain of gushing cold air and my leg muscles throbbed from exertion. The tiredness and pain helped keep my mind off being a loner.

Once in a while, I would somehow find myself with the loose football. Everyone would freeze waiting for me to get rid of it. No one spoke; they just waited. They acted like there was an impenetrable force between me and them, between their world and mine. To them, I simply didn't exist. Even the girls, who watched the boys play and rooted for whom they liked, echoed slowly to silence until I threw the ball to someone else. This just added to my embarrassment, and I would run harder to block it all out. The burning in my lungs would flow into my veins and swell them with throbbing pain and return to my heart in the form of scorching loneliness.

I should have learned not to care, but ignoring it wasn't an option. I had a consuming desire to belong and feel wanted. Those taunting questions would circle through my confused mind adding to my discomfort. *Why did I have to be here at all? Why am I forced to stay in this arena, surrounded by these solid, heartless gargoyles?*

At night, I had to go home and sleep in a dark, concrete walled basement. This just made me feel more the prisoner. My older brother and I shared a room with one small window. I felt uncomfortable in that room and would usually sleep with the covers over my head to protect me from whatever might be there.

One night, I awoke very suddenly. I had been startled by something not heard nor felt by normal senses. The room was dark. The house was quiet, no noise from upstairs. All were asleep. My sister was usually up till eleven or midnight doing homework. When her light was on, I could see it through my window. It wasn't on, so I guessed it was past midnight.

I had chills prickling my scalp, and my stomach was feeling light. I wondered what had brought me wide awake so abruptly. I looked to the foot of my bed, and there was an outline, a shadow with the form of a person wearing a derby-type hat. I couldn't see any distinct features, just a dark shadow. It began walking slowly toward the foot of my bed. With each step, it sunk lower into the floor. When it reached my bed, it vanished into the darkness surrounding it.

"Did you see that?" my brother whispered. "What was it?"

"I don't know," I quivered.

I pulled my blankets over my head and tucked them tightly around my body. Then I tucked into a ball as snugly as I could make myself. We never discussed the incident nor told anyone about it. The feeling wasn't unlike how I felt at school though.

## 7

*When you lie crushed and prostrate, bemoaning your fate*
*in pitiful*
*accents, will you hear the words 'O how brave a man!'*
*said over you?*
*If you are reduced to such straits no one will so much as*
*call you a man.*

—Marcus Tullius Cicero

I was tolerably miserable at school until around Halloween. One day after school, I was just getting onto the bus when someone grabbed me from behind and threw me to the ground.

"Hey, mama's boy," he taunted.

I looked up into a pair of small black eyes. This boy had jet-black hair, a dark complexion, and thick black eyelashes. I didn't know his name but knew of him. I had heard him one day bragging that he smoked and drank and would be a professional bank robber someday. He always had two friends with him whom he referred to as his bodyguards. Frequently, they would choose a prey, then pick on that person for a week or so. This was constant harassment. They would knock the book from his hands, push him, hit him, kick him, and be as obnoxious as possible.

"I want to fight you," he said calmly. This was just some game to him.

"I don't want to fight," I insisted.

He started pushing me, and his bullies moved close in.

"Don't bother this one," he commanded them. "I want to fight him by myself. If you'll fight me, I'll make them leave you alone," he promised.

By this time, a crowd had gathered. Many were cheering me on to kick the heck out of that bully. I was surprised that anyone would have more enemies than I did. Suddenly, I got thinking that if I won this fight, I might be accepted and gain some friends. I put up my fists. He hit me in the mouth, and it didn't hurt. This gave me more courage. I took a big swing that hit his chest and forced a grunt as air surged from his lungs.

The confident look he had been wearing was now a worried stare. I swung again, and my right hand glanced off his right cheek. He started backing up. I wanted to hurry and get this over with, so I quickly stepped in for another punch. He struck out and hit my forehead. Again, it didn't hurt. I moved in and hit him hard with a right to the left cheek. It immediately turned his cheek red, and I hit him again in the nose. I saw his eyes fill with water as the crowd became intensely loud. I knew he wanted to quit, but pride wouldn't allow it. I would have to whip him soundly to get him to back down.

All the cheering and ruckus died abruptly. The other boy looked past me, and his expression appeared to be one of relief. I braced for his bodyguards to hit me from behind. Instead, I saw and felt a large hand grip tightly onto my left shoulder. The fingers were long and fat. I hadn't seen fingers that huge before. With his left hand, he grabbed the other boy by the right shoulder. I looked up to see a heavyset, balding man. His face was as round as a bowling ball, and he scowled at me. His eyes were set too far back into his head, looking like creatures waiting to pounce from dark caves.

"Oh no, Jungle Jim," I groaned to myself.

He was the high school gym teacher, and many morbid stories had circulated as to his intolerance for fighting. I had heard that he once took a kid into a back room and beat him up with a tightly rolled and taped towel. I was scared to death of him before I ever saw him. Now he had a hold of me. My mind raced with horrible thoughts of him torturing me with barbells or throwing me into the PE dryer and watching me spin into unconsciousness.

"If I catch you two fighting again, I'll take you into my back room and beat you bloody. Do you understand me?" he roared.

Involuntarily, my head began nodding jerkily up and down. The muscles in my neck were trying to cut off my airway. I was gripped with a terror I had never felt before. I thought I would never fight again.

"I don't forget faces," he added as he lumbered back toward the high school.

"You're a lot tougher than I expected," the other boy complimented me.

As I was climbing onto the bus, someone touched my shoulder. He was a tall, thin, friendly looking boy whom I didn't recognize.

"You clearly won the fight," he stated. "He fights all the time and is tough. You beat him good."

I nodded acknowledgement and hurried onto the bus. I wanted out of there. I didn't like the fighting nor the attention. I didn't like Jungle Jim being able to recognize me either.

The next day after school, I ran to the basement to use the bathroom before boarding the bus. *What a dingy place.* It smelled like that stuff they put into toilets to try to keep a raunchy place smelling good. Concrete walls were painted lime green. It was more a dungeon than a bathroom. The urinal was one long trough. I hated that and only used it when no one else was around.

"How's our mama's boy?" a familiar voice interrupted my thoughts. "We're going to finish our fight down here where no one will break it up."

"And we're going to make sure he wins," his fat body-guard laughed.

He was the same boy who had given me problems with the lunchroom troublemakers. The other bodyguard was short and husky. He looked like one of those farm boys who fill out early from all the hard work they do.

"I'm not fighting anybody," I insisted.

"Oh yes you are," he yelled as he hit me in the mouth.

One of the bodyguards hit me in the back. While I gasped to breathe, the other boy hit me on the side of my face. The three of them punched and kicked till I fell to my knees.

"That's enough," their boss ordered.

One of them put a foot in my back and pushed hard forcing me face first to the floor. The impact with the concrete sent pain bouncing through my lips and teeth. My emotions began to swirl. I was lonely, helpless, and hated to be alive. I got onto the bus crying but aware of the dark stares of those around me.

At home, my younger brother strutted around declaring he would help me get them tomorrow.

"If you do, I'll beat the tar out of you," Mom threatened him. "Why on earth can't you stay out of trouble?" she sneered at me.

I told my brother to just forget it because I wasn't fighting anyone. I was horrified at the thought of Jungle Jim catching me fighting.

The next two days brought the same treatment from the boy and his bodyguards. As I tried to get out the door of the school, the three of them threw me down the basement stairs and beat me up. They put bruises on top of the bruises from the day before. When I got onto the bus crying, an older girl expressed her disgust at my being such a pathetic boob.

I begged for Mom's help, but she just ignored me. I pleaded with her to call the principal or have my older brother beat them up. She just ignored me.

On that Friday, I woke up sore and scared. I couldn't go back to school. I lay in bed holding my breath and blowing hard for a long time, then went and told Mom I was sick. She felt my forehead and decided I had a fever.

"Just go back to bed," she told me to my great relief.

I was happy all of a sudden. Mom and I made cookies together that day, and she acted extra nice. I wondered if there was something wrong with her.

My older brother came home from school saying he had taken care of the troublemaker for me. When he told me the name of the boy he had fought with, it was someone I had never heard of. No matter. There was an entire weekend between me and the cruel kids.

On Monday, I hadn't thought much of my enemies. I assumed they had seen my brother whip the other boy and would leave me alone. It wasn't so. After school, they caught me again. This time, they slammed me around against the walls and hit harder. It was by far the worst beating. I guess they had stored too much energy since their last escapade. I went home hysterical. I was sitting in a chair next to Mom and crying frantically, begging her to go do something about this situation.

"Oh, just ignore it," she said impatiently.

"How can I ignore it," I screamed at her. "There are three of them, and they beat me up every day."

I needed her help and kept begging for it.

Unexpectedly, my Dad came flying into the room. I hadn't known he was home. He grabbed my arms and, squeezing hard, lifted me off the chair violently.

"You damn baby," he cursed between gritted teeth. He slammed me against the wall. "If you come home crying again, I'm going to beat the hell out of you."

I stared into those cold, cruel eyes and could see the evil demons dancing joyfully. They weren't taunting and laughing this time. They looked lustful and bloodthirsty. They were getting what they wanted. I had never felt anything so dark and evil before in my life. When he threw me to the floor, I shot up running. Out of fear, I ran downstairs and crawled deep into a corner of my closet, closing the door tightly. I didn't want to see anyone or be seen. Those awful feelings of shame and loneliness overwhelmed me. I was confused and uncertain. Perhaps I really was the guilty party in this. I began to accept that I was really a bad person, but I still wondered why. I wished hard that I would cease to exist or die to punish my parents. I sat and tried to imagine a funeral service with me dead in a casket and them crying. I could never bring to mind a scene of them crying over me, however. They wouldn't do that.

The next day at school, the pattern changed. The bullies couldn't wait for their fun. The three boys attacked me during lunch. I was crying and screaming for them to leave me alone.

"You guys knock it off and get away from him," someone threatened. "If any one of you ever touches him again, you're going to fight me, and I won't quit until you can't move or breathe. Now get out of here."

I looked to see a boy that I didn't know. He had a very stout build and was my age. He was twice my size though. His hair was cut in a short crew cut, and he had an almost square face. There wasn't much neck between his head and shoulders. His face and eyes looked very friendly and kind as I stared at him.

"They won't bother you anymore," he promised. "They know I mean what I say."

"Thanks."

I was more grateful than I could possibly express.

"Why hasn't someone done something about them bothering you before this?" he asked.

"My parents don't care about it," I told him.

He invited me home to lunch. It was within walking distance from the school. A sense of obligation made me accept his offer. When we got to his home, he told his Mom I was the one he had been talking about. I hadn't realized people were paying attention to my problems. I had felt so alone I didn't think anyone noticed. I should have realized I was making such a spectacle crying that everyone knew about it.

I was very quiet and nervous at his home. I got the impression that his mother wasn't happy with him bringing me there. I was probably like a stray dog to her. She didn't need me around.

When we got back to the school, he told me that if anyone gave me any trouble, I could come to him for help. It's odd that after his being so kind to me, our paths never crossed again. I didn't speak with him throughout our school years, and I don't recall ever being in a class with him.

8

*If you would seek war, prepare for war.*

—Terry Pratchett

A strange and sudden change came over me. I feared my Dad but hated him even more. I didn't fear the boys at school anymore. When anyone looked at me or spoke to me, I was very aggressive and threatening in my responses. I didn't want or need anyone's friendship. I wanted to be left completely alone. I wouldn't even hang around my brother. If anyone bothered me, I would make them regret it one way or another, I decided.

I had a strange meeting at this time. A broad-shouldered farm boy with sandy, blond hair and a very cheerful-looking face approached me and asked for a fight.

"I don't think you're so tough," he quipped although with a smile. "One of these days, I want to fight you," he added.

Looking at him, I decided to ignore him. He had on heavy work boots streaked with dried cow dung. His clothes were stained and filthy, and his hands were callused and dirty. I guessed he lived on a farm where he put in long, hard hours. He was too friendly to be fighting. I shook my head and walked away without saying anything.

The remainder of that school year was a major transformation time for me. I isolated myself more but also realized that I didn't need to fear the kids at school anymore.

During the spring, the junior high had a music festival in which many other schools were involved. I was walking between classes when I heard a boy from a rival school ask someone to help him find a certain boy who was the consensus toughest in our school. Their top fighter wanted to meet him. I went to the place they had appointed for the meeting and hid behind a large tree. Soon the messenger returned with our fighter.

He was a popular boy by fear and by looks. Not a person in our junior high would even consider fighting him. He was average height with a deep, thick chest. He had a light complexion and was always dressed and groomed. His arms bulged at the biceps and forearms. His build wasn't from farmwork though. He was a city boy who had a father who was just plain big. This boy looked like he worked out with weights.

The rival boy was slightly taller and thinner but no less muscled. His arms were long but tight. He was also well groomed and dressed. He appeared to be from a wealthy family and a city kid too.

"I hear you're pretty tough," he quizzed our fighter.

"Oh, cut the crap. Did you bring me out here to visit or fight? Our chorus is about ready to sing, and I have to get back."

The rival boy put up his fists and stepped forward. All in a flash, our fighter started swinging hard and fast. Each of his five or six blows landed solidly on the rival's head and face with loud pops. I could see his eyes turn milky and hazy. He dropped to the ground without throwing a punch. His face was red and puffy with some large white knots peppered over it. His friends gathered quickly around, wondering if they should call an ambulance. I looked up, and our fighter was on a dead run for the chorus building. He had some singing to take care of.

All that day I pondered over the fight. The popping noise of punches landing rang through my mind. The way our fighter had handled himself was exciting to me. *Could I swing that hard and that fast? Would I even dare to try it?* I rehearsed the fight over and over in my mind. I knew no one else would protect me if I needed it again. If I could learn what I had just witnessed, I would be able to protect myself. It wouldn't take long for kids to know they'd better leave me alone.

The summer between the sixth and seventh grades was similar to the previous ones. A lot of time was spent in the mountains, fishing, hiking, daydreaming, and feeling better about myself. Often, I thought of the fight I had watched. I was one of the smallest boys in my grade, yet I still wondered if I could use that method to protect myself. I still had those apprehensive feelings about fighting, but I knew that if a situation arose where I needed to fight, I would. *No one had ever gotten in trouble for beating up on me, so why should I ever get into trouble for protecting myself?* At times, I became excited at the prospect of trying to fight the new way.

One Saturday, my parents were in the grocery store shopping. We kids had to wait in the car, as usual. While we were waiting, a couple of boys rode up and parked their bikes outside the store. They started walking inside, and one of my younger brothers hollered and asked if he could ride their bikes.

"No," they yelled as they ran back to protect their property. "You keep your stinkin' hands off our bikes."

"My hands don't stink," my brother replied as he stuck them under the smaller boy's nose. "I'm real clean, and I won't hurt your bike if you let me ride it."

"No, just leave it alone," he said firmly.

"Okay, jerk," my brother snorted.

The boys headed into the store and my brother jumped on one of their bikes and yelled at them, "Hey, I like this one. I think I'll keep it."

The bigger of the two came running and grabbed my brother's arm. A surge, a strange flow of heat poured through my chest and face. My jaw and arms tightened.

"You get your hands off him," I ordered.

Running toward him, I realized he was much bigger than I was. I looked up into his threatening eyes.

"You're not very big," he mocked me. "Am I supposed to be afraid of you?" he sneered boldly.

"I don't care if you are or not," I warned him. "You let go of him now, or I'll beat your face in."

I was barely aware of my confidence and lack of fear. I felt anger and almost hatred for this kid whom I didn't know. I knew my brother was wrong.

"Get off the bike," he growled, jerking my brother's arm.

Hatred burning through my entire body, I jumped at the big kid and swung hard. I had a gross urge to hurt him. No way was I going to stand by and let anyone pick on me or my brothers. My fist landed under his nose and knocked his head back sharply. Blood quickly began to flow from one nostril. He stepped back with a shocked expression and started stuttering, trying to say something. Finally, he yelled for his friend to call the cops if we didn't give back the bike.

"Come on," I told my brother. "Let them have their bike."

"Sure," he replied, throwing the bike to the ground and kicking it. "It's a piece of junk anyway."

I sat quietly in the car on the way home wondering about the fight. *Why hadn't the boy fought back?* He was a full head taller than I was and much heavier. He should have pounded me, but he was afraid. I could sense it in him. It was evident in his eyes. There was a lot of power in that hit, too. The impact had driven him back and drew blood. I was elated at the prospect of being able to protect myself from the bullies at school.

When school started each year, the canal became off limits to us. Much of our free time in the summer was spent there. We planned to spend our last day prior to school starting out on our surfboard and swimming. The canal water was ice cold, even during the summer.

When we would go to swim, it was always a contest to see who would dare get in first. Sometimes we left without swimming because no one wanted to get so cold. This last day before the new school year was one of those days. The summer had been cool with more rain than usual, and there was still snow on the mountains. There had been snowfall on the Fourth of July. We were standing around, daring one another, and I was close to the bank. Suddenly, my body jolted involuntarily and flew into the icy water. As my feet hit bottom, something sharp tore through the underside of my left foot. I came up gasping and furious. Where I exited the canal, there was a pool of blood. I felt a sharp pain and left a red stain each place my left foot touched the ground.

"You stinkin' jerk," I yelled at my brother. "I'm gonna kick your head in."

This was the brother just younger than I was. He usually grew a spurt and got my size, and then I'd grow a spurt and be a little bigger. He was always broader and more muscular than I was, however. We quarreled often but didn't fight that much. This day became a turnaround though. He puffed out his chest and dared me to hit him. The pain in my foot had surfaced those angry, hateful feelings, and I was ticked off at his snottiness. With the right side of my body behind my punch, I swung hard and forceful. The punch landed solidly to the middle of his chest. His chest seemed to give way under my knuckles, and he started gasping for air. His face turned various colors, and he looked sickly. I became worried watching him try to breathe. Air wouldn't force its way into his lungs. I was afraid he was going to die. He started sucking in short gasps and stared at me with tears in his eyes. We had never hit each other to try to really hurt each other before. I could see the feeling of betrayal on his face.

I wondered why I had reacted so harshly and blindly. It wasn't normal for me to act that way, but it had seemed a natural response for him doing what he had done to me. Though I regretted hitting him, I was surprised at how hard I had hit. It added a little more courage to my once fragile ego.

9

*The body seeks that which has wounded the
mind with love.*

—Titus Lucretius Carus

The first day of seventh grade was exciting for me. I had tried to choose clothes that would look in style yet still be conservative. I bought hair oil so I could keep my hair just right. I even had a pair of pants pegged and got black pointed toe shoes. I was going to fit in even though that style of dress was uncomfortable and idiotic.

During lunch hour, not long after school started, a large group of boys were playing keep-away football between two of the schools. I was leaning against a wall, watching. The side of the building was directly in the sun and was warm and comfortable. It was natural for me to be standing and watching. No one invited me to play, but I knew I would have been welcome had I chose to join in. A tall boy got the ball and started running with it. My brother kicked his foot, and he fell hard to the ground. He quickly jumped up and shoved my brother.

"If you want to play rough, I'll show you rough," he shouted.

Instantly, I was between them. He was well dressed but not so friendly looking. I studied his face and figured that he was a grouch because he was so ugly. Seeing that face in the mirror each morning would make anyone a grouch, a conclusion which I readily shared with the tall aggressor.

"You're too little to stop me from beating him up," he jeered at me, ignoring my insults. "As soon as I take care of you, he'll be next," he laughed.

I wondered if he might be right. He was much taller than I was with a very stout build. He had to have at least twenty pounds on me. His arms were tanned and solid looking. Blood vessels bulged along them into an upper torso, which looked well worked.

I didn't need to argue anymore. He had threatened my brother and me. My upper lip began to twitch uncontrollably, and my arms were shaking. I started swinging with all my might and as fast as I could move. A new source of energy was pouring through my veins. The pop of each landing punch spurred me on to hit faster and harder. I wanted him to feel real hurt and a lot of it. I wanted him to hurt badly enough that he'd never want to bother my brother or me again. I wanted this hurt to carry deep into his soul. These morbid desires drove me wildly on.

He turned away and ducked his head.

"That's enough," he pleaded. "I quit. I'm sorry."

He turned his back toward me. His left cheek was swollen and bruised. White knots dotted his face and forehead. Blood flowed down his lip and dripped to the ground as he bent over to keep it off his clothes.

My chest ached slightly, and my heart quivered as a stab of sorrow made me wonder if I had been right or not. I felt sorry for him. Boys had backed away from him looking as though by helping him, the same might happen to them. White shades of fear masked many faces as the crowd became deadly silent. I sensed something was very wrong about the whole incident. Nevertheless, I decided I was fully justified in what I had done.

School became different. One boy who had seen the fight admired what I had done. He was very tall and skinny. We became friends, and sometimes, I actually got involved in group conversations with other boys because of our acquaintance. This was a new and exciting experience for me. It was strange to talk and have people at school listen. I was surprised that just fighting could make this kind of difference. My new friend even talked to girls. I would stand concealed behind him with my knees shaking and hands trembling while they visited.

This made me feel so uncomfortable. I don't know why it would make such a difference, talking to girls or boys, but it did. The thought of talking to a girl was petrifying. For some reason, the old shame and guilt would rise up to torment my nerves around them. Perhaps in my own eyes, I was still a coward.

I didn't like to fight, but when I did, I would tremble noticeably before fights began. I wanted to be accepted by girls too, but I assured myself it wasn't possible. Knowing they had all seen me crying and abused had much to do with it. I was certain that they perceived me as a crybaby and a chicken.

I enjoyed watching them from a distance though. I loved comparing the creative and numerous ways of styling their long, colorful hair, the soft features, and feminine walks and talk. Though I knew I couldn't be personal friends with any of them, I had respect for them and daydreamed about being accepted socially.

There had been much talk about my fight. Too many boys had seen it for it to be passed off as a fluke. Though others didn't try to become my friend because of it, many began to display a silent respect. Some even moved aside in the crowded halls to let me have a clear path. What a difference this was. It brought some happiness and satisfaction to my life.

Not many days after the fight, a boy hollered, "Hey you."

I turned to see the grubby farm boy. He wore heavy boots with dung on them, and his clothes were stained.

"I still want to fight you one of these days."

I smiled and went to class.

On Valentine's Day, my new friend asked me to deliver a valentine to a girl he liked.

"She goes to church with you," he informed me.

I'd never heard the name, but said I'd deliver it. We had youth meetings on Tuesdays, so I decided to give it to her there. It should have been a simple task but turned out to be very difficult for me. On Tuesday, I asked a boy to point this girl out for me.

"You like her?" he asked.

"I have no idea who she is," I said. "I don't think I've ever seen her before. A friend asked me to give her something for him."

"Well, she doesn't always come, just every once in a while," he told me.

After scanning the room, he pointed her out. She had pretty sandy hair put up in a ponytail. I loved ponytails. The hair pulled back let light sparkle across her face and forehead. Her nose was long and slender and ending with a slight bulb. That looked cute. Her eyes were blue and bright, highlighted with a little makeup. Her lashes were long and stiff and her brows light and blending into her complexion. Even though she wasn't smiling she looked as though she was. It was easy to see why my friend liked her. She probably had a bunch of male admirers.

She was standing with a group of girls. I started for them, but as I neared, I suddenly froze. My face tightened, and heat began climbing in a steady wave from my chin to my ears. I couldn't imagine a way to start a conversation with her. I didn't know how to talk to girls. *What if I said the wrong thing and made her mad?* I had an older sister, but we were like brothers to each other. She hunted, fished, swam, and climbed trees with the rest of the boys. These were two different categories of girls. Finally, I decided to get my brother to make the delivery. I was too scared and very outnumbered. One on one, I might have been able to deliver it but not with all those other girls there.

"Hi there," a soft and pleasant voice interrupted my concentration. How kind and gentle it sounded.

The girl I was supposed to deliver the valentine to was looking at me and leading her group toward me. I tried to mutter a hi but just emitted some *glub* sound. I smiled. My face was burning up. *Why had I allowed myself to get into this?* My stomach was light and uncomfortable, and my chest was beating a warning signal.

"I didn't know you came to church here," she added.

"My name is—" I began.

"I know who you are. I know all the good-looking guys," she cut me off. "Why are you so red? You're not shy around girls, are you? I'd never have thought you to be a shy one."

*Who was she talking about?* I guessed she had me mixed up with someone else. I didn't know her. In fact, I didn't really know any girls at school. Her shyness remark had fanned the fire in my face. It was so hot I could feel sparks popping on it. I was getting a headache, and stars began darting in front of my eyes. I looked at the girls behind her. None smiled nor even blinked. Seeing them reminded me of who I was. I was supposed to be a nobody. I quickly handed the note over.

"My friend asked me to give this to you," I wheezed nervously and hurriedly made a clumsy retreat.

The girls were all giggling, and I felt like an idiot. They were back there, laughing at me. I couldn't believe I had let myself get into such a humiliating situation. All the old feelings of shame and guilt I had acquired swarmed over me. I hurried home, got into bed, and hid under my covers.

Pondering over it all, I had enjoyed the situation a little. That sweet voice had pulled away walls enclosing me. I wanted to talk and visit with that girl more. She had been so kind and complimenting. Absolutely no one had ever treated me that way before. I tried to plan how to handle the same situation in case it happened again. If I got another chance to talk to her, I didn't want it to be so short. I wrestled myself to sleep trying to grasp her calling me good looking. *Was she teasing me or just starting a conversation?*

The next week, my friend gave me another note to deliver. I was anxious but afraid. I wanted to see that girl and hear her voice again. I loved seeing her smile and feeling that electrical charge as she talked to me. I wasn't sure I wanted to face the embarrassment though. In spite of my mixed emotions, I spent the entire day impatiently waiting to get to our youth meeting that night. I planned every step and every word carefully.

By the time I got to church, I was too excited to go in. I wanted to see her outside before the meeting and before any of her friends were around. I waited anxiously as each of her friends came by and went into the building. When she didn't show, I became heartsick and felt slightly abused. *Why had she been so nice and then not shown up this week?* I wondered if she were some new kind of tormentor sent to make my life more confused and miserable. She probably knew how vulnerable I was and was mocking and hurting me with fake kindness. Flashes of past abuse darted through my war-torn mind. What a jerk I was. I was meant to be a loner and shouldn't fight against it. Besides, if I wanted to avoid being a target, I must learn to keep myself out of sight. I was too mortified to stay at church. I needed to go learn how to fight this new kind of bully. I couldn't beat her up. I didn't even want to. Girls were different than boys and should be treated as such. They were a special part of our society and usually the best and gentler side of it. Even though I sensed that this was true, I certainly hadn't experienced it.

Instead of going home, I just sat outside sorting through an array of twisting and dizzying emotions. I concluded that I should have known better than to get sucked in. I was dealt a blow because I opened myself up and just stood there taking it. I wasn't supposed to be likeable, and I had let hope climb over my defenses to disarm me.

After the meeting, I waited for my brothers to come out so we could walk home together. One of the girls came out, saw me, and started walking toward me. She had a blank look on her face, and her eyes were fixed directly on me. Her stare wasn't a bit friendly. I looked behind me to see if she might be looking at someone else. No one was there. Worry sizzled through my mind. Fear crawled across my skin, leaving chilling bumps behind it. *What had I done? Was I going to be the target of a girl's wrath now that I had earned some measure of respect from the boys?* I prepared for a mother-like scolding, one of those that made me feel shameful and wicked. I must have done something stupid that had offended the other girl the previous week. Maybe she hadn't come to church because of me.

"Man, I've been lookin' all over for you. You skipped out on the meeting, huh?" she scolded. "The girl you're playing cupid with for your friend asked me to tell you she was sorry she couldn't be here this week. I don't see why, but she said she had looked forward to seeing you."

Expressionless, she turned and marched stiffly away.

I was bewildered. *How could she have been thinking of me? Why would she be thinking of me?* More confusing was that she had been so kind as to send a message to explain her not coming. She must really be different than other people. Just as quickly as my emotions had entangled in hurt and confusion, they now swept me with anticipation and excitement. *How could I have doubted her? She had been so nice.* This was a terrific feeling, thinking that someone might actually like me. The fact that it was a girl was more exhilarating than anything else. I found another of her friends and gave her my buddy's note.

The next week, I had another note to deliver. My friend was curious as to why he hadn't received a reply to his solicitations. I assured him that I would find out. My emotions were hovering out of reach. I was nervous, scared, and excited. I was lonesome being so excited and unable to tell anyone about it. I had to share my elation with myself through fantasies and daydreaming. I traveled deep within my mind to lose the time of day. I was too anxious for that evening to come. Even Christmas had never felt this way before. I worried about how excited I was. I might not act normal feeling this way. *What if I acted like a dope and chased her away?* I really longed for a true friend, whom I knew liked me.

At church, I waited impatiently again. Each of her friends came through the door. *Would she ever get there? What if she didn't come again?* The agony and delight fought delirious rounds with each other inside of me while I waited and hoped. Delight suddenly landed a knockout blow. Here she came, jerking the door open so friskily, bounding and smiling over to her friends. I tried to go to her, but my legs wouldn't move. My feet disobeyed my orders, and a warning alarm was ringing in my ears. *Why hadn't she even looked my way? Was all this really just a fantasy in my mind?* I thought of the embarrassment I would have to tangle with if I were overstepping reality. But I did have a note to give her. That gave me a good excuse to go talk to her. Again, I sent orders, and my body wouldn't respond. *Why couldn't I move? How could fear have such an overpowering hold on me?* My eyes froze to the back of her head. I measured the distance between us. It couldn't be more than eight to ten steps. I worried that someone might be watching me. It was getting too hot. Sweat was splashing my face and body, fighting the fire that furled my emotions. I needed a place to hide. The boy's restroom was just a few feet away. I decided to turn and make a dash for it. This was no longer fun; it was humiliating. As I started to turn, she glanced back at me. I smiled a forlorn smile and tried to go. My body still refused to be obedient. She squinted her eyes with a look of concern, then turned and came over to me.

"Are you sick?" she asked in a sincere tone.

*Boy, was I ever.* My throat hurt, my feet throbbed, and my head was tight and sore. I was exhausted.

"Why didn't you come and say hi?" she asked expectantly.

"I…I…I'm fine," I finally squeaked out a stammered reply.

"Boy, you really are nervous around girls, aren't you?" She giggled. "There's nothing to be afraid of," she chided, "but I think it is so cute."

"No, it's not that," I fibbed. "It just seems to be awful hot in here."

The heat began to intensify again.

"I have another note from my friend. He wondered if you would write him back," I finished.

She smiled and then looked strangely serious.

"Speak for yourself, John," she said quietly.

My heart sank.

"But I'm not John," I protested, realizing that she must really have mistaken me for someone else.

She had started to turn away. She smiled and winked a message that was beyond comprehension.

I lay awake for hours that night trying to untangle the mess of cobwebs in my head. *Was John someone I knew or was supposed to know? Was I supposed to write her a note? I could never do that! My friend had written three and received no reply. That kind of rejection would be too much of a blow to my already low self-esteem.* I wondered laboriously for days then weeks over her calling me John.

During this time, my friend had given up on her, and I was content with a smile and a hi each time I saw her. It was nice to be liked by someone. It helped my confidence having a girl not be afraid to be seen talking to me. None of her friends would talk to me or even smile at me. They just stood back like some side ego being bruised each time she spoke to me. Their animosity and cold glares were discomforting and kept me from being too well acquainted with my new friend.

I started wondering again what it was about me that brought on such threatening attacks. These girls' silent criticisms were just as harmful to me as had been the physical ones by the boys in previous years. I tried to avoid eye contact with anyone in the halls in order to prevent new misery. I spent hours trying to pinpoint what it was about me that was so unattractive. Even with the nice girl, I couldn't help but wonder what her motive for kindness was. There must be some adverse reason for her sudden attraction to me. This suspicion constantly rattled and hissed warnings of caution inside my mind. It was a constant fight to keep these suspicions caged and unexpressed.

10

*Now, what would I want with a reputation?*
*That's a good way to get yourself killed.*

—James Garner

Though my fight had brought me some offbeat sort of respect, there were some doubters. Once in a while some bigger kid would make a remark about being tougher than I was or that I didn't need to think I was hot because I had won a fight. Mostly, I just ignored them. One particular boy wouldn't let it go though. He was an Indian who was living with a farm family in our community. Over about a three-week period, he kept telling my brother that he wanted to fight me. I just ignored it until he came up in the hall and pushed me

Immediately, a rage stormed within me. *Why would he bring attention to me?* I didn't want people looking at me. I drove hard into his chest with both the palms of my hands, pushing him against a wall. He banged against it and grunted from the impact. I stared into his threatening, dark eyes. The shadows there were different than Dad's. His were more serious and hateful looking. An urge began to swell within me. I wanted to start swinging and pound furiously at those shadows. I needed to beat away the evil radiating from him.

A crowd had already gathered. I didn't want or need the attention, not from students and, more importantly, not from teachers. I walked away, my face tight, my heart racing. Inside, I was erupting with bitterness and embarrassment. All through the next class, I felt flushed, and my mind raced over and over what had happened. *What did those who had seen the incident think of me? Would this make me more unpopular and bring on more attacks?* I worried over it torturously. *Why hadn't the fight at the first of the year put an end to this kid of garbage?* I hated the thought of having to fight again. I was sure this kid would be back to finish what he had started. I wouldn't and couldn't back down anymore. I began to shake thinking of the upcoming battle.

After school, the Indian was waiting outside. Most of the people around our area felt sorry for the Indians. They did what they could to help them. I had nothing to gain from fighting him and risked a lot of wrath if I beat him up. I loved to read Indian stories. I admired the wild instincts and courage their leaders had possessed. These factors all weighed heavily against me fighting him. The positive factor was that I wouldn't let anyone push me around anymore. This boy had been in other fights and had a reputation as a tough kid. Now he was waiting for me to fight him. I went straight to him and told him if he insisted on a fight, it would have to be where no one else was around.

"I just want to hurt you," he said pointedly, agreeing to my terms.

My brother saw us heading behind the school and followed. As I rounded the building, the Indian pulled a knife from his pocket.

"I want to hurt you bad," he repeated. "I hate you, and I am going to hurt you."

My brother grabbed him in a tight chokehold and demanded that he drop the knife.

"If you're going to fight, it's going to be a clean fight, or I'm going to help," my brother warned him.

"Okay, I'll fight clean," the Indian responded.

A chill began to climb my back and face; goose bumps dotted my arms. I guess by hurt, this guy must mean kill, literally. I wasn't sure I was ready for this. My fighting was for protection and to convince others to leave me alone. I didn't believe in trying to kill, maim, or in any way seriously hurt anyone. Using weapons, kicking, and anything other than just fists seemed so cowardly and dishonest to me. I wondered what it was going to take to end this fight.

"Let's fight," he snarled. "You hit me now because you won't have another chance."

He wasn't as tall as I was but certainly more muscular. His clenched fists rippled the brownish skin with waves of well-toned muscles. I knew my physique wouldn't impress anyone. I was short and thin. His taunting had renewed the anger in me though. I decided I had to teach him a lesson no matter how it hurt me. I threw a punch, which he blocked quickly and ducked under. He held one forearm horizontally in front of himself and moved it up and down to block punches. This looked weird to me.

"You can't hit me through my guard," he bragged. "A good fighter at home taught me this. You can't hit me, but I will hit you." He put a heavy emphasis on "will."

I had no more respect for him. Indian or not he was a braggart and a troublemaker. Worst of all, he was forcing me into something I hated. The rage surged through me, and I started swinging. My knuckles were pounding against solid bone. I could hear the hollow smacks as punch after punch landed hard around his head and on his arms. I tried to swing with more force to drive his arms into his face as he used them to protect himself. The emotional flames were flaring higher and higher within me, erupting more energy into each swing. My legs tightened and began to move me instinctively, keeping me in contact with this retreating target. I had not thought of time or whether I would tire. The furnace burned hot and could supply all I demanded. He lunged forward and wrapped his arms tightly around me. All my energy was pounding in thin air. He tripped me, and I tried to turn, so I would fall on top of him. His grip, however, was tight and controlled. He drove me back down. I landed hard on his hands, sending an excruciating pain up and down my spine. Air was forced brutally from my lungs, and my head banged against the ground. My vision and mind instantly filled with darkness. Large, bright lights began darting in scattered directions throughout my brain. My lips and fingers were numb, and my arms and legs weakened quickly. Lying there, I felt my strength flowed away like water, spilling on the ground. There was a dull ache in my right cheek as my head was driven again to the earth. I knew he had hit me, but I felt little pain from it. I couldn't see a thing except the darkness and flashing lights. I could hear clearly though. As his punch landed, he screamed in pain. I guessed my landing on his hands had probably hurt his wrist or fingers. I heard my brother threaten him to let up and fight fair or he would step in.

"I can't fight anymore," he shrieked. "I just hurt my hands."

I heard him groaning in pain as he left. He didn't come back to school; he had gone back to wherever he came from. The only lingering effect of the fight for me was a very sore bruise on my back. I hated fighting and decided I would avoid it at all costs.

Some stories circulated around the school as to the Indian's leaving. One was of a gang beating him up. Another was that he'd gotten homesick. The most prevalent was a warped version of what had actually happened. It rumored that my brother and I had beat him up. The family that he had lived with had a girl my age who was very kind and always smiling. Many kids at school who were her friends felt her loss needed avenged. Various threats were delivered to my brother and me, but nothing ever came of them.

To me though, this was a harsh judgment again. No one asked me anything about it. They just made their own judgments, and I was guilty. The bitterness of the whole affair left me drained. I couldn't feel happiness or joy in anything. My life was so gray and dull. All feeling and emotion was bound and blunt. I became more aware of those around me. Everyone had friends and joked and seemed to have fun. Again, I began to wonder and grope, trying to see what was wrong with me. *What made me so different? There were kids at school I could easily like, but everyone should be likeable to someone. What could make kids so totally despise me?* Even adults were starting to treat me as though I were a plague. The boy I did hang around with didn't really seem like a friend. We were more a convenience for each other than friends.

The rest of the seventh grade was about normal for what had been normal for me. I was often surprised that I could be around so many kids and yet go so unnoticed. Sometimes it was eerie. I was in a world of zombies. At least when they walked by me that is what they seemed to be. At recesses, I still stayed to myself while the others played football or whatever. Even in the classroom, I was a nonentity. Teachers often called on other quiet or nonparticipating students, but they didn't call on me. When he handed out papers, they called kids' names to come get theirs, but with mine, they would become silent and just walk over and give it to me. They seemed afraid to say my name.

I frequently could hear Mom's voice echoing through my hollow mind telling me to just ignore it all, but I didn't know how to do that. For hours, I waded through my tangled thoughts fishing for a connection to bridge me to the world around me. So often, I would feel hauntingly alone and lost, lost in a whole town full of people. All this mental hunting and searching would leave me weak and with thundering headaches. In the most desperate times, I would yearn for someone to sit down and talk to and laugh with. These mental desires would flow through my winding veins to pool up in a lonely heart. It would cry out an expression of desolate misery heard by no one and felt by no one but me. The roots of my emotions would absorb the misery and force it from unwilling eyes. In the form of small teardrops, the misery would shower an ever so tiny speck of earth, my small portion of a dark and shadowy abyss. Thinking of the girl who had been so kind to me would often let in a ray of hope, but I dared not to test that kindness, fearing that in its depths it would be so icy cold. These wondering times became too exhausting. I tried to find ways to dam them up before they could overflow. I started chastising myself for being so weak and babyish. I had to learn to walk through this darkness without fear or hope. It was my dark forest, and I must learn to live in it with all its grave, dark shadows.

Close toward the end of the seventh grade, I was at a scout day with my brothers. It was being held at a church near the school. I was watching a group of scouts build a rope bridge. My brother came and told me some kid had been picking on him and that the boy wanted to fight me. Emotionless, I followed him to where the kid had said he would meet us.

As we approached him, my brother hollered and said, "Here he is. Now let's see how tough you are."

My heart crawled into my belly as I neared him. This was obviously another one of those overworked farm boys. He had huge arms and legs, was well tanned, and was much taller and wider than I was.

*What in the world is my brother trying to do to me?* I wondered. *This guy will probably tear me to pieces. Maybe my brother is mad at me for something, and this is his way of getting even?*

The other boy looked at me and blushed.

"I didn't say I wanted to fight you," he said matter-of-factly. "But I'm not saying I'm afraid of you either."

He was speaking calmly, but there was a slight hint of uncertainty in his voice.

"I don't see how anyone as small as you could be as tough as your brother says you are, but I'm not curious enough to find out."

I was very relieved. I didn't say a word. I turned and walked away. As we were leaving, my brother hollered back at the kid, calling him a chicken. I was tempted to reach over and hit him.

A short time later, another brother came up to me crying. He said some big kid had been picking on him. I erupted into a shower of rage this time. I hated people picking on other people, especially if it was one of my family. When we reached the school playground, he was pushing around a friend of my brother's.

The bully was about my height but was two and a half times wider. His arms looked like the clubs cave men carried. He was a bit on the plump side but more solid than fat, one of those kids who looked fat because of how big they are but still muscular. He was another farm boy. I knew of him because he rode our bus sometimes. He was usually suspended from riding the bus because he liked to pick fights. Up close to him, the first thing I really noticed was his hands. They were huge. They reminded me of my Dad's sledgehammer.

*Man, I'd hate to be hit by those*, I thought.

"Is this the shrimpy dork you brought to protect you?" He laughed at my brother. He reached out and shoved my brother on the ground.

The volcanic eruption hit its peak now. My ears were hot, my scalp tightened, and rage flowed through the rest of my body. I lunged forward and shoved him full force. I fell backward, and he didn't move a bit. I was too angry to let that influence my desire to hurt him. I jumped up and started swinging fast. He was too slow to even come close to swinging and hitting me between all my blows. I could feel and hear the pops as my fists hammered time after time on his face. He began back-pedaling, but I kept up with him.

A large crowd had gathered by this time. With all the pounding on his face, I thought he would have given up. I paused a moment to see if there was any sign of surrender, but he didn't say anything. I was about to start swinging again when I felt a soft touch on my shoulder. I looked behind me, and there stood a very kindly looking lady. She was pretty and had long, dark hair and dark eyes. She spoke with a soft and gentle voice.

"We shouldn't do that here," she said with sincerity. She still had hold on my arm very gently as she asked us to please stop fighting. She was too kind for me to even think of saying no.

"Sure," I said, responding to her influence.

I turned to look to my opponent for his response, and he reached up and hit me in the mouth. The blow lifted my upper lip into my nose, bloodying both. My eyes filled quickly with water, and a ripping pain knifed through my torn lip. My tongue jumped instinctively to check the damage, and I could feel small shreds of torn flesh hanging loose. Blood was already etching a stain down my shirt. The lady gasped in shocked disbelief at the cowardly attack.

"Oh, I am so sorry. I was holding your arm, and you couldn't even protect yourself," she apologized. "That was an awfully cruel thing for him to do."

The apology doused some of my pain. I felt a tingle of happiness thinking that someone actually cared that I had been hurt. I wondered what it would be like to have a mother who cared like that.

I looked for my attacker, and he was running across the playground. I had no desire to chase after him. Looking back at the lady, she had tears running down her cheeks. I felt more sorry for her hurt than for my own.

"Come to the church and let me help you clean that up," she offered.

An electrical pulse ran throughout my body as I thought of her actually touching me. I was happy and excited, and as much as I wished for her to help me, I felt it would be too abusive of her and too sissy for me to allow it.

"Thanks, but I'll be all right," I told her.

I didn't feel any of the pain as I watched her leave and wished I could go with her and just sit down and talk. On the way to the bathroom, her face and voice replayed over and over through my mind. I wondered though if she would have been so nice if she had known who I was.

11

*You pierce my soul. I am half agony,*
*half hope.*

—Jane Austen

At one of our youth meetings, the nice girl kept looking at me and smiling. Throughout the evening, I could feel I was being watched, and each time I looked, she was staring at me. She always smiled and occasionally winked. When the meeting was over, she signaled for me to come to her. I was excitedly nervous, wondering what she wanted me for. The darkness of my world gained color and light from her cute and kind manner. Instantly, a magical door opened and let out all the negative and hurtful feelings that were trapped inside me. If she wanted to see me, it didn't matter what others thought or did. What a terrific feeling this was. It reminded me of the nice lady on the playground. I looked at her again, eyes twinkling happily, her smile a radiation of light and joy, and a face that reflected inner peace. Her dainty finger was motioning slowly, beckoning me to come to her. I don't know how I got to where she was because I felt no contact with the floor. I just floated gently to her. It all seemed in slow but distinct movement. All my senses opened wide and released years of confusion. Her perfume freshened my mind as it swept sweetly through my nostrils.

She giggled and bade me to follow her down the stairs to a dimly lit basement hallway. Heavy chains that had held me bound in a darkened cell fell helplessly from my soul. I was brought into the light by a soothing voice leading me into a dark passageway. Even as others controlled life with the cold stone walls they put between me and their world, now she controlled it by leading me as a child into a new world.

"Do you remember when I said to you, 'Speak for yourself, John,'" she asked softly.

"Yes," I answered puzzled.

"Well, don't you know what that means?"

"No. I thought you thought I was somebody else," I replied.

"You're funny," she teased. Then she told me some story about a guy named John who was trying to get some girl to like his friend, and she had told him to speak for himself.

I had never heard the story, but I got the gist of what she was saying. Thinking about it caused me to blush enough that it was noticeable in the dim light. Not knowing how to respond to her story made me blush even worse.

"My, you are changing different shades of red," she said, enjoying my embarrassment. "Do I make you nervous, or are you embarrassed because a girl told you that she likes you?"

I didn't mind the embarrassment in this situation. It was so soothing just to hear her talk. It didn't matter what she said just so she talked. Even though I was very hot and perspiring, it was the best discomfort I could know. I got the empty feeling in my chest, and my heart beat briskly. I wanted to tell her that I liked her too, but I couldn't formulate any coherent expressions. *What was I supposed to say in a situation like this?* I had no idea. I began to panic and perspire more. If I didn't say something, she might think I didn't appreciate what she was doing and saying. I opened my mouth to speak, but my words were prisoners. There was no escape for them. I blushed again nervously.

"You're really new at this, huh?" She kindly helped out. "I like the way you look and blush like that."

More compliments, more embarrassment, and more fear.

"I…I've never heard that story before," I stammered.

"You understand what I'm saying, don't you?" she quizzed.

"Well, yes…no…I mean…I guess I do. No one has ever liked me before."

I agonized over how to please her. I feared that admitting to her that I felt she liked me would be degrading her because of who I was. No one was supposed to like me, especially girls. I felt so hopeless and trapped, but I wanted to be in the trap. I didn't want this to ever end. It was far more pleasant than the freedom of my everyday life.

"Will you call me?" she requested.

"Well, we don't have a phone, but I would like to call you."

She put her hand on my arm. The soft, cold fingers sent chills quickly across my skin. My heart sped up, and another flush ran across my face. I wanted to reach out and touch the back of her hand, but again, fear stopped me cold. That might be too forward. I must be careful to keep her friendship; it was as precious as pure gold.

"Hey, come on," someone interrupted from the top of the stairs. "If you want a ride, we're leaving."

I looked up to see one of her friends.

"Keep in touch." She smiled and winked. "Girls aren't supposed to be so forward, but since you're so shy…" She smirked.

I grinned and blushed again.

"Sure, thanks," I replied awkwardly as she hurried up the stairs.

What a great feeling. I hated dancing, but I nearly started dancing on the spot. My emotions were erupting again, but this was a Fourth of July celebration. Having lived under the gaze of dark shadows for so long brightened this even more. I spent the whole night awake replaying that moment with her, and yet I got up early the next morning refreshed and happy.

When summer vacation started, one of my brothers found a new pastime. He had been at the canal and seen some friends floating on inner tubes. They told him a person could float for miles. There were numerous headgates along the canal, which let water into ditches. At these places, the water would become very swift with waves. This offered great excitement, and we spent much of our time floating from our house down to the highway than walking back again.

Frequently, during the summer months, I worked for local farmers doing different jobs. Sometimes it would be hauling hay, others irrigating, and sometimes burning weeds. One afternoon when I got home from hauling hay, a brother told me they had gone up the canal about a mile and a half that day to float in their tubes. There was a gravel pit full of water next to where they got into the canal. It was deep enough to dive into, and the water on the surface was warmer than the ice-cold canal.

"Yeah, and some girl was there and said for you to come see her and swim when you're not working," one of the younger brothers added.

They started teasing me about having a girlfriend. I wondered if this was the girl I hoped it was. I hadn't known that she lived so close to us. *Why hadn't she told me where she lived? She probably thought I knew already.* We often rode our bikes for miles around there, and I had ridden by her home many times. Of course, it wouldn't have made much difference if I had known she lived there because the thought that her parents might be there would have prevented me from stopping.

The next day, the hot, heavy work seemed easier than usual. As small as I was, the hay bales didn't weigh much less than I did and sometimes even more. Anticipating going to the gravel pit pushed my adrenalin to the limit though, and I worked hard to finish that particular haying season. When the day came that I didn't have to go haying, Mom had made a big list of work for me to do around the yard. Our family always grew a huge garden and canned food for the winter. I liked having the garden, but I didn't like keeping it weeded. Watering was okay, but weeding was awful. We had a pasture to feed our cow, and the pasture grew thistles by the thousands. We had to constantly keep those cut too. Along with these was all the general irrigation and yard work. I worked fast and hard on this special day so I could get out of there. As quickly as we boys got our work done, we shot off before Mom could give us more.

I wanted to run all the way to the gravel pit, but my brothers kept hollering for me to slow down and wait for them. We got to the pit at about 12:30. My heart sank when I saw she wasn't there. I had built up too much of an expectation. When we looked over the edge of the pit, the water was calm, green, and reflecting a glaring light into our eyes. A crude wooden raft floated lazily out in the middle. A taunting silence echoed across the rock walls—no sound, no movement, no people. The disappointment kept an annoying ache in my chest as we swam, dove, and sat on the warm rocks to get heat back into our chilled bodies. Again, doubts tried to infiltrate my mind and sabotage my emotions, but past experience now rose to force me to confront the situation rationally. She didn't know anything of my being out there that day. She couldn't be out there all the time waiting for me to show up. Besides, I had never called her. I could have used a pay phone. The trouble was I was just too afraid to call. I felt most secure to just let chance dictate life.

On the surface, this water was warmer than the canal. Below the surface, it got much cooler. The deeper we swam, the colder it got. With my eyes open, I could see nothing as I swam into the darkness. Looking back though, I could see the light shining from the surface behind me. At the very bottom, the water was icy and black. I liked to kick hard off the rocks and move fast as I could to the top. There was something about the darkness and the unusually cold water that kept drawing me back to the bottom to explore what I couldn't see.

As I surfaced from one of my dives, I heard a familiar voice. "Hi there, good lookin'."

In the midst of the cold pond, a wave of heat scorched my face. I appreciated her greeting, but I knew once we got home, my brothers would razz me about her calling me good looking. This would start the rest of the family in, and they would all tease me incessantly. Oh well, I was too warm inside right then to let that bother me.

"Why are you always blushing?" she mused. "It doesn't figure you being so sensitive and having such a rep as a fighter."

That drained the blush from my face. The cold of the pit was able to crawl through my skin and start me shivering. I didn't want her to think I was mean. I wasn't mean. I was no bully. I just couldn't let others bully me around and had to act mean to keep from being picked on all the time. Of course, she couldn't understand that. She was a girl. Size and strength weren't as a much a factor with girls as they were with boys.

"Why don't you come over and sit by me? I can't get in the water for a half hour after I eat, and we just had lunch," she explained.

A shock stiffened my body and let me sink. I got a little water in my mouth and throat and surfaced choking. A fire of emotions burned through me. *Would I dare to sit by her? Was it even proper? How could I talk her out of it?* I hated, loved, feared, and desired to be close to her. Then I looked up at her and saw what I hadn't noticed before. Not only was her voice different but so was her body. I felt ashamed for noticing it. *What if she realized I had thought that?* She would probably hate me. She just looked a lot different in a bathing suit. My shivering doubled as nervousness added shaking to shivering. I was swelled with a surge of excitement, a yearning to be near her, yet an alarm ringing a warning that I was stepping out of bounds.

I started to doggy paddle as slowly as I could toward her. I looked up at that cute, smiling face and felt like a fish being reeled involuntarily toward the shore. I really liked her, not the way I liked football or the way I liked milk shakes I bought every time I had extra money. This was so very different. It was sort of like climbing a high peak and looking over lakes and vast ranges of beautiful mountains. It was a thrill that exhilarated the emotions I always tried to hide, those which showed I was happy, friendly, and harmless, the ones of peace and freedom.

Now I wondered, *Who am I supposed to be when I'm around her?*

"Are you a bad swimmer, or don't you want to come over here?" She dove into my thoughts.

I had an excuse, but I was too scared to talk. If she knew how afraid I was of sitting by her, she would probably laugh to death. I just looked at her and smiled as I climbed out of the water.

"Come sit by me." She patted the ground right next to her.

"I sat down a little further away from where she had patted. I didn't even dare to look at her. *What if I couldn't help looking at her suit?* As I had sat down, I noticed that it was slightly revealing at the top. She might slap my face if my eyes were not well behaved.

"Boy, you are shivering terribly." She gasped. "Here, wrap my towel over your shoulders."

"No, that's okay," I replied. "I always shake like this, but I warm up fast."

*Boy, what a lie.* I was scared to death. I couldn't wrap a towel around me that had touched her. The thought seemed immoral to me. My nerves were popping at the ends. No situation I had ever been in had made me feel so strange and uncomfortable.

Soon, the rays of the sun and the warmth of her kindness had reheated my body. The shaking persisted, however, especially when she scooted over closer and touched my arm.

"Tell me honestly," she said. "Are you afraid of me?"

Her tone had a serious nature to it, which I had never heard from her before.

*Why does she always do this to me?* I thought as I blushed red-hot again.

"Well, yeah, I guess I am a little," I replied staring at the water.

There were ripples reverberating out away from the shore, and there were ripples sending shockwaves through me.

"What do you think I'll do to you?" she asked more teasingly. "I've never seen anyone blush so easily and often as you do. I just really think it's cute."

More heat rushed my face as my body quit shaking. She laughed sweetly, which put me more at ease.

"You blush and blush over blushes. I hope I don't scare you so you won't come back and see me again."

"No, I like to talk to you," I quickly assured her.

I wanted her to be forward and open like she was. I would certainly not become friends with a girl who wasn't that way. I couldn't. I would never have the nerve to start a conversation. All I knew of conversation was to say hi and blush.

"Why do you look away when you talk to me or when I talk to you?"

She had a way of asking questions in a funny way. It seemed like a game almost. I could feel myself being propelled form my dark world up into the bright sunshine. I loved this about her. She let me be so peaceful and free under her spell.

"I don't know," I said as I blushed again.

"Don't you like to look at my beautiful face?" she joked sarcastically as she threw her head back and pulled her hair to one side.

"Yes, I like to look at you a lot," I told her seriously.

She sensed the tone of my response and smiled without replying.

"Well, I guess it's safe for me to swim now. Shall we?" she offered as she dove into the water.

When my brothers and I dove, we had our arms wide, legs bent, and jumped hard making a big splash. She looked sleek and graceful, hands and legs straight and together. With a gentle hop, she went up, bent beautifully at the waist, straightened her legs, and entered the water without much more than a ripple. It was so fun being there with her. A soothing warmth radiated through my body thinking that she just might really like me. I still couldn't allow myself to know it was real though. Not even my dreams were ever this pleasant.

Over the rest of that summer, I went to the pit as often as I could. Sometimes she'd be there, and sometimes, to my heartfelt disappointment, she wouldn't. I always hoped for the chance meeting.

## 12

*The spider spreads her webs,*
*whether she be*
*In poet's tower, cellar, or barn, or tree.*

—Percy Shelley

The eighth and ninth grades were basically the calm before the storm. With a few exceptions, these years were pleasant, and I was accepted by most students. Even popular kids would say hi to me once in a while. I still didn't interact extensively but would be with groups of boys as they discussed important things such as girls, motorcycles, cars, and sports. I was relaxed most of the time. This led me to become more interested in grades, athletics, and school activities. I even helped decorate for a couple of dances. This was the crowning point of my acceptance. Not many students were asked to help decorate for dances. I would feel a slow unknotting of my emotional confusion. I even wrote a book during this time. It was a kid's mystery. I let one of my brothers read it and then threw it away. I knew that writing a book would overstep the bounds and bring back the cold days. I was certain my parents would think it was foolish also. The ambition was there though. I built carts and toy boats and experimented with different things Mom had in the cupboards. I just felt creative and wanted to learn. In my English classes, I even thrived at writing short stories, which brought praise from my teachers. Usually this praise was in front of the class though, which I hated. I knew that when I blushed, I looked like a bright, red tomato. I didn't like that sort of attention. I did however like the praise from the teachers when they would write notes on my papers saying how they enjoyed my stories. In my ninth grade algebra class, I was even asked a question during class. This was something I had never done before in class. It embarrassed me so bad that I never made that mistake again. Having the teacher and all the kids in the class looking at me was a bit much for my tattered ego.

In the eighth grade, I was most surprised at the attention I received from the girls. Quite often, a girl would say hi to me when I passed her in the hall. Even the most popular girls would speak to me occasionally. I had to guard against letting my joy show through at such attention, but I sure walked above the floor at times. I even looked at the kids instead of looking at the floor or walls. In classes where guys would group together to discuss boy stuff, I was invited into the conversations. Frequently, I didn't like what they talked about and especially the way they talked about girls. No girl warranted disrespect, and I hated the filthy way they expressed their purpose for having girlfriends. One boy in particular was worse than the others. He constantly told of immoral excursions with various girls. He was the same boy who had given me all the trouble in the lunchroom in the fifth grade.

During the middle of the school year, he began going steady with a girl a year younger than us. She had a sister who was our same age. My cousin, who lived with us was going steady with the other girl. He, my brothers, and I often went to the girl's house to listen to music and have pizza parties. Word got around to her boyfriend that I was going with this girl while he was also. This was not true. I enjoyed visiting at their home, but I always pushed off her attempts at snuggling. I didn't like it, nor did I like the stories her boyfriend had told of the things they had done together. His exploits with her, by his account, were extremely immoral. Various people would let me know that she was deliberately using me to make him jealous. Because of this, I quit accompanying my cousin and brothers to the girl's home.

One night at a church dance, this girl was there and asked me to dance with her. I didn't want to, but it felt rude to say no. We danced, and she apologized for using me. She told me that she really liked me much more than she did the other boy, and whether I liked her or not, she would break up with him. I didn't care for her telling me all that stuff but told her that I considered her a friend. Even that made me terribly uncomfortable, and I began to sweat excessively. I could feel the wetness between our hands and all over my face and arms.

"You feel awfully warm," she said. "Should we go outside?"

"No," I replied quickly. "I have to go home early, so I need to leave."

As I walked off the floor, she followed. When I got into the hall leading up the stairway to the outside door, her boyfriend was there.

"I was just comin' to get you," he growled. His two sidekicks pushed me into a room. As they did, my brother saw the commotion and followed.

"You better stay out of this," he ordered my brother. Looking at me, he added, "This is just between you and me, man to man."

I almost laughed. He certainly was no man. The way he talked and acted at school, I figured him more pig than person. I didn't like the squirrelly dork, and I was really glad to get this opportunity. He talked, dressed, and acted like he was some important hoodlum out of the movies.

"Shut the door," he commanded one of his thugs. "I don't want Mommy's boy runnin' out on me. You keep that door blocked until this fight is over."

Turning to me, he pulled a comb from his pocket and combed back his greasy hair.

"You ain't walkin' outta here 'til I'm done with you, and when I'm done with you, you won't be able to walk at all," he snorted.

He reached out and pushed me. I wasn't expecting it and backed into a chair and fell onto it in the sitting position. I hurriedly slid to one side and flew to my feet. With both hands, I hit him hard in the chest, sending him flying against the wall. I started swinging and could feel the blows crunching on his face. This was one person I had a good reason to fight and wanted to fight. No amount of hurt could be too much for him. Maybe I could teach him to mind his own business. I pounded harder and quicker. The room was too small for him to go anywhere, and it had enough chairs set up in it to make the fighting area even smaller. This kept us in real close quarters. He tried to swing, but my blows pounded back his arms. He tried to back up but would quickly run out of room, and I would be immediately on him swinging as fast and as hard as my body could deliver the power.

I didn't feel the anger and hatred I had felt in other fights. Those were driven by rage. This was driven by sheer desire. I just wanted to hurt this weasel, and I was happy to have the privilege to do it. Everything around me moved in slow motion. I could see him and my punches meeting each other. Each time he moved, I could react as if he were restricted by the slow motion and I wasn't. I had him against a wall, and when I hit him, his head bounced off the wall giving double the punishment. He ducked, and one of my punches landed on the wall, but it didn't hurt. I brought an uppercut from below him and lifted him back upright. He was just there, like a helpless target. He was one of those dark shadows except with a real body. I worried that he might fall and end my fun. With his head up, I could see that filthy mouth and focused in on it. I wanted to pound it shut. Then I wouldn't have to listen to his garbage at school. He tried to turn away, and a hard right and left sent him down onto the same chair he pushed me onto. His head was jerking helplessly from side to side as I hit him with one hand then the other. I just kept going because he needed it. Maybe this would knock some sense into him. I heard my brother tell someone to just stay back and let us go. I figured his punk friends were thinking of grabbing me. I swung harder. I wanted to make sure he learned before we stopped. I had a strange tickling inside me as though my spirit was dancing and rejoicing. I wasn't tired. I hoped his buddy would grab me to give me a reason to get even with him too.

I felt a hand on my shoulder and quickly turned and knocked it away. I was expecting to get hit and was ready to duck and punch. Instead, I looked up into the face of the bishop.

"I'm sorry," I sputtered. "I thought his buddies were going to gang up on me."

"What's this all about?" he demanded.

"His friends pushed my brother in here and shut the door so Slicky could beat him up. But he ended up getting whipped," my brother explained.

"That doesn't surprise me," the bishop answered. "He seems to always be causing trouble. You go ahead back to the dance," he told me. "He won't be giving you any more trouble tonight."

Slicky's girlfriend stuck her head in the door and threw a ring at him.

"I don't want anything to do with you," she sneered.

The girl I had hoped to see at the dance hadn't show up, so I went home. I had only gone so I could see her. I began to wonder if maybe that was why I wasn't afraid of that fight. I really didn't enjoy fighting, and I figured this one would cause enough stink that I'd never have to fight again. Looking at Slicky, I thought he had just paid the penalty for whom I had wanted to be at the dance not being there. He had big knots all of his face and forehead. His mouth and nose were bleeding, and he looked to be in a lot of pain. Those marks would be there the next day at school and probably a black eye. I knew too that his ex-girlfriend would spread this all over the school with some exaggeration. I hoped this would remove the rest of the dark that still hung over me socially.

13

*I don't see how you could ever be
anything but mine.*

—Kenny Chesney

As I left the dance, I was overcome with an empty feeling. I had looked forward to seeing that girl who was always nice to me. It meant everything to me. Just seeing her at school or driving around town or anywhere brightened my moods. I would feel a heat of emotion rush through me, giving me goose bumps each time I saw her. I wished I could be more outgoing so I could develop our friendship better. I still felt guilty about this though. I was sure that being more forward would be stepping out of line. I feared what kids at school would say if they saw me talking to her too much. I feared for her losing friends and being treated as I had been. I also knew that I would have to put up with horrendous teasing from my family, especially my father, if I had a girlfriend. She had written me a few notes and had chastised me for not writing back to her. I was too embarrassed to give her a note, so I wrote one and stuck it in her locker when no one was around. If that got into the wrong hands, it would ruin me. I couldn't stand the embarrassment of kids knowing I had written a note to a girl. I just couldn't allow myself to be as close to her as I wished I could. This seemed quite offensive to her.

"Are you ashamed to be seen with me?" she asked me one day at a noontime dance.

"No," I replied. "I'm afraid of it. I don't know why, but it scares me a lot to be around a girl in public. I guess I'm afraid of being made fun of or something. I don't like feeling that way because I really like you a lot, way more than I can tell you. Besides, I worry that you will lose friends if you are seen with me too often." With that, I could feel the blood rushing to my face again.

"Oh, blushing again." She giggled. "You are really a strange person. I would be offended by anyone else acting that way toward me, but with you, it's different. I know you truly are shy in a crazy way. Well, at least you will dance with me, right?" She grabbed my hand. This was a fast dance, and she knew I hated to fast dance. I felt so foolish and knew people would laugh at me. That I couldn't take.

"When there's a slow dance," I protested.

"Come on," she insisted as she pulled me to the dance floor. "Just try it at least once, okay?"

I gave in, and the flush rushed to my face again. I dreaded this and immediately began to sweat heavily. There weren't that many kids dancing, which made it all the worse. I had nowhere to hide on that dreadful floor.

"Oh please," I begged her. "Let's wait for a slow dance."

I got sick as I tried to move my arms and legs, but they were frozen sticks in a cast iron frame. Sweat was pouring down my face, arms, and body. My blushing had reached a new dimension that made my head feel as if it would burst wide open. I began to gasp for air.

"I can't do this," I squeaked out.

She began to laugh. "You do look really funny."

I was stunned. *How could she insult me like that?* I was mortified. She was making fun of me. I hurried off the floor. I wanted somewhere to hide. I was sure everyone was looking at me laughing. I was bombarded with humiliation. For the first time since I had known that wonderful girl, I welled with a bit of anger toward her. She had made me a target and let me get hit solidly. When I looked around, no one was looking at me. She was still on the floor dancing. My stomach was churning violently, and I sat down to regain self-control. I became very upset at her. She must have been lying to me all along just to get the chance to humiliate me in public. I wondered if I had beaten up someone she liked and she had done this to get even. How terribly cruel she was.

A slow dance started, and she ran over quickly. She bent down and grabbed my hand.

"Come on. You owe me a dance." She smiled. "This will probably be the last dance today."

Her hand was small and soft on my fingers. Her smile was kind, and her request to dance with me was sincere. She tugged gently to urge me to follow her. From where she was touching me, a stampede of ticklish sparks ran up my arms and across my body. This was a wonderful healing sensation. I wanted to dance with her so I could be close to her. We went to the floor, and I carefully put my left hand on her side. She reached around and pulled it tight across her back.

"It's okay if you hold me a little tighter," she spoke softly, staring into my eyes.

When I extended my right hand to her left, she pulled them in close to us.

"It feels better this way," she spoke softly and in such a delicate tone that I dared not back away. I was blushing harder than ever. I wasn't sure this was proper. I mean, I wasn't sure I should have felt so excited about it. It wasn't just that I was this close to a girl. It was that I was this close to a girl I liked more than I dared admit to myself. The warmth of her body flowed through me like rays of sunshine. I was sure that I ought to feel wicked for enjoying her touch, but I relaxed from the pure pleasure of it and wondered if she could possibly be enjoying the dance as much as I was. If she felt the way I did, I shouldn't need to be closed and shy around her. I wasn't sure that that was a good idea either. I wondered if other kids were watching us. *What if one of my brothers was watching?* I could tell my body was trying to blush, but something else fought against it. This wasn't a time for that. She laid her head gently to my chest, and a bell rang. I didn't want to let her go. I wanted to hold on forever. I realized that this was a person who really did care about me. As far as I could tell, she was the only one in the whole world who did. This made her all the more special. Shadows just couldn't hit me with her around. I wanted to think that I needed her, but I couldn't quite allow it.

I started to carry her books to class and spend lunch hour with her and other such fun things. I was extremely nervous knowing others were seeing us together so much, but being with her was so fulfilling that the emotions drawing me to her outfought the ones pushing me away. I found myself wanting to do things because they made her happy. It didn't matter how I felt about it. I could handle some embarrassment if what caused it made her happy. I got razzed at home a bunch about her too. I found, oddly though, that I could mostly ignore it. Besides, I wasn't about to change the situation. I was rich—rich with something more precious than money. Nothing I had ever bought had made me feel the way I did with her. I was beginning to think that I might just be normal after all.

# 14

*Not that I hope, (for, oh, that hope were vain!)*
*By words your lost affection to regain;*
*But having lost whate'er was worth my care,*
*Why should I fear to lose a dying prayer?*

—John Dryden

Toward the end of the school year, we were having an afternoon dance at school. The kids I was friends with started to egg me about asking someone to dance. We looked at different girls and talked about some for a while.

"Hey, let's go ask a girl if she wants to dance, and if she says yes, let's say, 'I hope somebody asks you,'" my friend suggested.

"We could probably get some weird reactions." I laughed.

"Okay, let's do it," he said as he scanned for a victim.

I didn't want my girlfriend to see me ask someone else to dance, so I decided to pull a stunt on her but quickly let her know that I was joking. When I started walking toward her, she left her friends and came toward me.

"Want to dance?" I asked.

"Of course," she replied.

"Hope somebody asks you," I said very quietly.

I didn't think it was even loud enough for her to hear. I was reaching for her hand when it fired out and slapped my face. She hit hard. It hurt more than any hit I had gotten in any fight. I wondered how those small hands and arms could hit so hard. I was bewildered.

"I was just kidding," I protested. "Me and my buddy just wondered what kinds of reaction we'd get."

"I know you were kidding," she said sternly. "But that is a very cruel thing to do to a girl. Some girls could be terribly crushed by such a mean joke. I can't believe that you would even consider such a thing."

"I'm sorry," I told her. "I didn't think about it before I did it, or I wouldn't have done it at all. Would you please dance with me?" I begged.

"No," she shot back firmly. "I'm not going to talk to you again until I think you have paid for that disgusting joke, and that won't be for a long time."

I became choked in bewilderment. *How could life change so suddenly?*

She stomped back to her circle of friends while I stood looking after her. I was sure she would change her mind. Her friends all turned and glared at me. I couldn't figure out how something so trivial could get such a reaction. Girls certainly were different than boys. If a joke like that were played on a boy, he would probably just laugh. *How was I supposed to know how girls would react, actually, way overreact to that situation?*

I found my friend and told him what happened.

"Yeah, mine started crying," he said regretfully. "I even tried to apologize, but she wouldn't let me."

"We made a stupid mistake," I told him. "But how could we know girls would act like that? I was really gonna dance with her."

After school, I tried to carry my ex-girlfriend's books to the bus. She jerked them away and, without a word, stomped off.

"That wasn't very nice," one of her friends said from behind me. "Your friend hurt another girl's feelings really bad."

"I know," I answered forlornly. "We didn't mean to be cruel. We were going to dance with them. I didn't think for a second they would get so upset."

"You sure are stupid," she quipped. "She was nice to you when no one else even liked you. You at least have a few friends because of her. Well, you had a few." She snorted as she turned and walked away.

I couldn't eat supper that night. I was sick and empty inside. Mostly I was sad thinking I had hurt her feelings. All the ill will I had felt toward other guys for mistreating girls and now I had done something so mean. What a scum I was. It was all right if people didn't like me for being me, but I hated that I gave others and myself a real reason to look down on me. Even the older kids had heard about what I had done that day. I was a criminal. The whole world wanted me to suffer for some stupid mistake that wasn't even my idea. My sister gave me a stern lecture about abusing girls' feelings.

"Girls are very sensitive," she scolded. "What you did today was horribly embarrassing to the girls you did it to."

I didn't want excused for what I had done, but I wondered if it was so embarrassing why the girls spread it around so much. *Everyone makes mistakes, so why wasn't I allowed to make one without being so persecuted?*

I didn't sleep very well that night. I dreaded going to school. *I was sure I could handle myself if boys picked fights with me, but what if all the girls started coming up and slapping my face?* The night dragged on long and slow. I got up tired and foggy when morning finally came. I thought about faking sick just to give the whole thing a day to blow over. Mom didn't buy it, however. I went out to the milk cow and slipped on the way back to the house. I fell, spilling all the milk onto the ground. Mom chewed me out angrily for that. I fell asleep trying to eat breakfast. The next thing I knew, I was being rushed out the door to catch the bus. I got a lot of strange stares from kids as I filed to the rear, looking for a seat. I wondered why they were all staring at me that way. Maybe it was because of the garbage at school the previous day. It didn't matter to me then anyway. I was too tired to care.

"You look a mess," my sister whispered to me. "Why didn't you at least comb your hair?"

So that was it. I had forgotten to clean up. I probably smelled like a barn, too. I dozed off without giving it too much thought. At school, my brother shook me awake to get me off the bus. I looked into the cold eyes of the bus driver.

"Come on. Get off the bus. I've got to get to work," he bellowed at us.

Inside the school, I didn't notice anything around me. I was exhausted. It was surprising how much energy could be spent worrying all night and how tired it could leave me, but staying awake all night because of something exciting didn't. I usually didn't go to bed past nine o'clock, and I almost never stayed awake all night.

I stumbled to my locker in a fog of confusion. All the noise around me seemed distant and echoed through my clogged mind. The lights were blurred, and I was ready to sleep. I opened my locker and hung my jacket up. Then I took off my shirt and hung it up. As I turned to undo my belt, I heard a gasp, which startled me. A girl was standing there watching me undress. A quick rush of heat sent an alarm ringing through my brain. I grabbed my shirt and put it on quickly, then turned and ran to class. I hadn't recognized the girl who saw me, but I worried all day about her telling the whole school of what I had done. Two stupid acts in two days like that would probably put me back socially where I had started, if I wasn't there already. I spent a miserable long day with worry choking all my feelings. When it finally ended, I was greatly relieved that nothing out of the ordinary had occurred. When I got to the bus, I thought of how glad I was that school for that year was almost over.

15

> *But true expression, like th' unchanging sun,*
> *Clears, and improves whate'er it shines upon,*
> *It gilds all objects, but it alters none.*
>
> —Alexander Pope

During the summer, our church had a big youth outing in the mountains. I hadn't talked to my one-time girlfriend, who seemed to hate me, for a long while. I hoped desperately that she would be at the outing. If I could be alone with her in the mountains, I was sure I could get her to forgive me. I needed her friendship.

The boys' groups weren't allowed to camp within three miles of the lodge. We were to camp in the mountains that night and go to the lodge for games and fun the next day. After our camp was set up the first evening, a group of boys asked me to go with them to the lodge. They had girlfriends there whom they wanted to see that night. They intended to spot where the girls were camped while it was light, then go back to visit after dark.

*What a great chance for me to see her again,* I thought. *Maybe if I showed up with the others, she would be more forgiving.*

Then my mind filled with all the negatives. *What if she slapped me and screamed for me to leave? I'd get caught and get us all into big trouble. She might even put me down miserably in front of everyone. She knew how easily I was embarrassed.* I decided not to go, but I hurt with the desire to see her and talk with her again. One of my brothers did go with the band of marauders though. They were gone 'til way past dark. I had begun to worry about them. These mountains were steep and covered a lot of area. If they got lost, it would be a cold and scary night. When I finally heard them, they were running and laughing hard as they dove into their tents.

"What's up?" I asked my brother. He was out of breath and quite excited.

"We got to the lodge and found the girls before dark," he explained. "But our girls were sleeping in the lodge instead of in tents. When it got dark, we snuck inside their rooms while the counselors were having a meeting. We were visiting and telling stories when a girl from another group came by and saw us. She started to scream, so we had to jump out the windows to get away. One of the boys with us landed crooked on an ankle, and we had to carry him most of the way back. Then when we were almost here, we just about got caught again. Those idiot women counselors came out in their cars looking for us."

I wanted to ask if my friend was there but decided I'd just wait for the next day. I'd probably sleep better not knowing one way or the other.

We were up and packed early in the morning. Everyone was going to eat breakfast together at the lodge. I got nervous and shaky anticipating getting to talk to her again. Surely, she would have forgiven me by now. I had suffered much more than she could have realized. This had been worse than if my best friend had died. In this situation, my best friend was there all the time, but I couldn't talk to her or have any contact at all.

While getting my food, I saw her friend who had chewed me out for being so stupid. She was serving the hot cakes. I loved hot cakes and wondered if she would give me any. When I got near her, she saw me and scowled.

"Hi," I said as I smiled at her. "Did your friend come up with you guys?"

"What's it to you?" she snarled back. "She wouldn't talk to you even if she was here, which she isn't. Her mom wouldn't let her come because there would be boys like you up here."

I quickly lost my appetite. For the first time in a long while, I actually wanted to cry. I was all alone back in that dark and ugly world. I ate a few bites of my food and had to throw the rest away. That was hard for me to do because we never wasted at home. Mom always told us about starving kids around the world and how they would love to have a tenth of what we had. That didn't bother my brothers too much, but it had a profound effect on me. I couldn't waste without thinking of some poor skin and bones kid having nothing to eat.

The best attraction at this camp, other than the girls, was a slide that was about thirty feet high. It ran down a steep slope and really flung you at the bottom. There was plenty of sawdust and sand to help break the fall when you landed. While waiting for everyone to finish breakfast, a bunch of us were having a contest to see who could land the farthest away from the slide. Everyone was anxious to get a lot of tries at it before a big line formed and before we had to go do all the dumb stuff that the adults had planned for us. One of my brothers was just in front of me. As he hit the bottom, I pushed off hard on the rails to get up good speed. I hadn't watched him clear out of the way. When I looked up, he was still on the ground. I quickly grabbed the outside of the slide with both hands and squeezed hard to slow myself. Kids were screaming for my brother to move. My stomach wrenched with twisted nerves as I thought of what would happen if I landed on him. While I was trying to see a way out of this mess, I was gripped with a shredding pain in my right thumb. I was moving so fast, and it happened so quickly that I figured I must have scratched it on a piece of loose metal. At the bottom of the slide, I dropped my feet quickly and dove sideways to avoid a collision. My hands hit hard in the sand and sawdust, and a renewed burst of pain in my right hand forced out an involuntary shriek.

"Oh shoot, what happened?" my brother gasped, looking at my hand with wide and wild eyes. A couple of girls standing close by screamed and turned away.

I looked down to see what had them all so upset. There was blood splattered all over my hand and arm and a small pool forming on the ground. A deep gash was flowing a steady stream over my palm. A meaty piece of flesh hung loose and visible. Some boys grabbed me and started helping me up the hill toward the lodge. The wound was throbbing and firing pain up my arm almost intolerably, but I made a resolve not to cry in front of anyone. It was difficult not to, but knowing the girls were watching locked my tears inside. My mind became hazy and numb. I weakened going up the slope. What little I was aware of around me seemed to be spinning and floating up and down causing more discomfort to my stomach. I was glad I hadn't eaten much. I knew I couldn't have kept it down. As we neared the lodge, I heard a lot of gasps and shrieks from girls. Their cries bounced nauseatingly through my head and made my hand hurt worse. One of the lady counselors took me into a bathroom to "cleanse the wound," as she put it. She ran cold water over the gash and rubbed and dug to get out the sand and sawdust. When she had first taken hold of me and talked so kindly, it had calmed me a little. I immensely enjoyed those feelings I got when nicer ladies were kind to me. But this cleansing routine hurt worse than ever. Each time she touched the cut, my stomach tightened, and heat and sweat flooded my face. I could feel a sickening numbing as she rubbed her fingers on the open flesh. Tears started to seep into my eyes. The pain was too great for me to put much effort into not crying. The tears slowly built up and broke loose, splattering on the edge of the sink.

"You're not going to pass out on me, are you?" she asked with a worried look on her face. I looked into her eyes. They were brown and soft. She spoke caringly and had a very kind face. Her sweet voice soothed my pain and helped me relax. She reminded me of someone else being kind to me, but I couldn't remember who. My mind was flashing sharp messages through my head, and I was losing strength in my arms and legs. I tried to answer her but could barely get my head to shake no, as a calming blackness built and swarmed over me and instantly the pain was masked in a peaceful drowsiness.

"You boys grab him. Don't let him fall," the lady abruptly directed the boys who had brought me to her. Suddenly, the pain shot back sharper and sent shocks to further parts of my body. I looked into the open cut and could see jagged peaks of meat where the blood had been cleaned away momentarily. Then like a flowing river, new blood wound its way in and around the jags until the wound was covered with blood. I turned my head away and saw that the doorway to the bathroom was jammed with kids standing on tiptoes trying to get a peek at what was going on. It embarrassed me, and a hot flush rushed me as I met their eyes. The lady put a compact on the cut and wrapped it with gauze to hold it in place. I was then taken to my scout leader's car. On the way there, I saw the hot cake girl.

"Serves you right, jerk!" she sneered.

"Is that a friend of yours?" one of the boys asked sarcastically.

I was driven to a doctor's office in Harden. There we met my Mom. She watched the nurse unwrap and remove the dressing.

Seeing the cut, Mom told them to get it sewed up so she could take me home. She was her own matter-of-fact self. I wanted to tell her how horribly it was hurting and throbbing, but I was sure she would tell me to ignore it. I didn't want to hear that, so I said nothing. I watched the doctor sewing the cut. He remarked on how good a job was done cleaning it out. As he pulled the cut closed with each stitch, I could feel a dull pain in the numbed hand. It sent a wave of weakening nausea through me.

"You better turn your head away, son," the doctor suggested. "You look like you may pass out. We wouldn't want a bump on our head to go along with this nasty cut, now would we?"

I was too sore and too tired to answer. I just wanted to lie down and sleep.

At home, Mom told me to go rest. I went to the couch and drifted off quickly. I was awakened by some giggling and talking, which I knew was not family. When I opened my eyes, I was blanketed with the familiar flush of heat. I had heard something about being so cute sound asleep like that. *There she was. How could they be so cruel as to let her in to see me this way?* I felt stupid and babyish. I quickly sat up, putting my weight on my bandaged hand.

"Ouch," I screamed.

"Don't get up, good lookin'," she said sweetly.

I enjoyed hearing that voice again. *What a heavenly blessing.*

"I heard you got wounded and just wanted to stop by and check up on you."

My brother had gone into another room with a friend who had come with her. I was glad they were gone so I wouldn't be more embarrassed.

"I just wanted to come and let you know I care," she added. "And to see you blush again. You don't have to feel like it's sissy for me to see you hurt."

"Well, I wouldn't want you to think—"

"I know how you think," she cut me off. "You're so weird. You're afraid I would be showing you pity, and that's not manly, is it?" She started to laugh.

I hoped she would stay for a long time. I loved the happiness that overwhelmed me while she was around.

Her friend came into the room with my brother. She was a nice-looking and very shy person. My brother liked her, but she made no attachments to boys. She seldom would talk to any.

"I'm sorry you got hurt," she sympathized.

I blushed from her being nice to me. I felt so foolish.

"Thanks," I said.

I tried to stand up, and all went black. I fell uncomfortably back to the couch.

"You don't need to get up, tough guy," my friend insisted. "I have to go anyway. My Mom is expecting me home." She turned to leave, and sadness crashed into my heart. I yearned to visit with her and hear her talk and laugh. She hadn't even left, and I was torn with loneliness.

"Oh, by the way," she added as she headed for the door, "I really do care, but I'm still not going to be speaking to you. You haven't paid for what you did."

"But I'm truly sorry," I pleaded.

She smiled and walked away. Now I was really confused. *How could she come and be so nice and yet supposedly be angry with me at the same time?* It hurt my head as I tried to puzzle it out. I went to sleep craving her company.

# 16

*Let my soul dwell with Common Sense.*

—Thomas Reid

When the ninth grade began, I was comfortable with my life. I still had friends. People weren't picking on me, and teachers acted as before, like I wasn't even around. This was fine with me. It was convenient that way. I didn't have to worry about being called on and having unwanted attention drawn to me in class.

There was a major change, however. I had always been small, but now I was even smaller. I was walking around in the shadows of trees. I hadn't grown much and weighed just over ninety pounds. Many of the boys at school had grown considerably in height and weight. I was grateful that I didn't have to worry about fighting anymore.

The kid I had run around with in the seventh and eighth grades lost his mom to cancer partway into the school year. His Dad worked road construction and was seldom home. These circumstances brought about a marked change in his personality. He became more aggressive with others but closer to me. We hung around a lot more and became better friends. He also lost some of his self-restraint. His mother had been a very kind and religious person. She had had a good effect on him as far as morality and clean living go. Now, he began to talk more vulgar, tell crude jokes, and smoke a little.

In our health class one day, he tapped the girl in front of him on the shoulder.

"Hey," he got her attention. "What's six inches long, has two nuts, and makes you fat?"

"I don't care," she scowled back at him.

"An Almond Joy bar," he teased. "Do you get it?"

"Shut up, pig," she snapped back.

"That's not very nice," I whispered to him.

"I know, but she knows what I mean," he said loud enough for her to hear him.

I didn't appreciate his joke at all, and I told him after class.

"Aw, I heard she's been sleepin' around," he said. "She'll think about it and think it's funny."

"I don't even think it's funny," I said flatly.

He promised me he wouldn't repeat the joke again.

The principal of our junior high was a man we called Snort. He was as wide as he was tall. Our school was a square building with a gym floor in the center and classrooms around the sides. Snort allowed no horseplay in his school and tolerated no misconduct. During class changes and at lunch time, he would stand in the middle of the floor, arms folded, and watch threateningly for any breach of his rules. He had no neck, and his head appeared to turn completely around. He was built like an owl except plumper. He also had a large paddle with holes drilled in it, which I had seen him use. It had Board of Education written in large red letters across the front of it. I was sure I didn't want him to know who I was, and I never wanted to have any close contact with him. I knew that any meeting with him would be unpleasant no matter what the circumstances.

During PE one morning, we were playing softball. One of our school bullies was in the class. He enjoyed walking by kids and hitting them in the crotch. If they protested, he hit them in the mouth. I never saw him hang around with anyone. I think the reason was a combination of his not wanting friends and no one wanted to be his friend. He was a stocky boy, mean looking, and real short tempered. While my friend and I were waiting in line to bat, the bully walked by my friend and slapped him in the groin with the back of his hand. My friend bent over in pain. I was instantly fused with the boiling rage, which now gripped me so frequently. I grabbed his shirt and pushed him against the backstop.

"You even think of doing that to me, and I'll bust your face, you jerk," I warned him.

His eyes were wide, and I knew I had caught him off guard. He stared coldly at me and told me he'd see me at noon out on the football field. That field was directly in front of the school where most everyone played during lunch. It was easy for the teachers to keep an eye on and see all that went on.

"What's the matter, chicken crap?" I prodded him. "You want to fight out in the open so Snort can stop the fight, don't you? I'll meet you behind the school with no one around. That way I can do a good job of busting your face without interruption."

I was scared and mad at the same time. I'd seen him hit people, and he hit hard. I began thinking more about what I was doing.

"What's going on over there?" the coach demanded.

"Nothin'," the bully replied. "We were just talkin'."

"Well, pay attention to the game," the coach ordered.

At noon, the bully didn't show, and I was glad to let it drop.

When the high school started wrestling, I just happened by the open gym door on my way home from school. I had missed the bus. One of the wrestlers was sitting out on the steps cooling off.

"Hey, what grade are you in?" he asked me.

"Ninth," I replied.

"How much do you weigh?" he added.

"I guess around ninety-five pounds," I told him. "Why?"

"Come try out for the wrestling team," he invited. "We don't have a ninety-eight pounder. You could wrestle varsity."

I went in and watched the practice for a while. I wasn't sure I wanted to wrestle. It didn't look fun to have one guy mauling another. The coach eventually came over and introduced himself.

"Why don't you take off your coat and shoes and try wrestling a few rounds and see what you think," he challenged.

I figured I was pretty tough and that I could beat some of his boys before telling him I didn't want to wrestle.

The first guy I wrestled was about my height but heavier built. He grabbed me and pinned me before I knew what was going on. I blushed quickly. I couldn't let it go there. With the next guy, I worked much harder. It took him quite a bit longer to pin me. While wrestling this time though, I realized that he moved me where he wanted me by using pressure on certain joints. By doing that, he countered my efforts to out muscle him. With the third guy, I was confident and perhaps caught him off guard and pinned him in a fairly short time. The entire team had been watching quietly, and the pin set them to buzzing. The coach had the first guy come back and started us again. I was breathing hard, but my adrenalin was also going. I needed to get even with this one, and I worked very hard. He threw me down quickly, but I immediately rolled to get on top. I used what leverage and strength I could but he had some quick and slick moves which made it hard for me to keep him down. If I countered one thing, he would go quickly into another move and soon was on top again. I hurried to stand up, and as I did, I threw my head back and hit him in the mouth. He let go, and blood was spattering the mat.

Two of the wrestlers, who looked huge to me, came and introduced themselves as the team captains. They said that they would personally see to it that I learned enough moves to become a good wrestler if I would join the team. I had no idea why these two would be so nice to me, but just because they were, I told them okay.

The next day in PE, the coach told the class that there were no freshmen on the wrestling team and he would give an automatic

A to any freshman who joined the team. I was glad I had made the choice to wrestle. Just for being on the team, I had already gotten an A on my report card. As were something that I seldom got.

The night of our first match, I was engulfed in fear. I was sure I would be embarrassed in front of all those people. I couldn't stand that. Plus, they always put the varsity results in the newspaper. Everyone in the town would read about me being pinned in the first round. And worst of all, a certain girl would know about it and think I was a wimp. My stomach hurt so badly that I couldn't stand up straight. No matter how many times I used the bathroom, it felt like I still had to go. I was so weak that even if I were a better wrestler than my opponent, I doubted I could do anything with him. I was bouncing around trying to settle my nerves a little when I stepped in something and almost fell. I looked down and realized that I was sweating a puddle on the floor. I became furious with myself for letting me get into such a horrible situation. What an idiot I was.

A junior on our team had tried to lose weight to get to ninety-eight but couldn't make it. There were, however, two sophomores who were there, including the boy whose lip I had split with my head. Once I joined the team though, these guys quickly became easy to beat. Now I wondered if maybe they just let me win because they knew how sick it made a person to be on varsity and get all that attention. Here I was, the idiot, in front of our whole town, our first match of the year, and I was the first one to wrestle. If I had dared, I would have told the coach that I was too sick. The thought of the attention that would bring prevented me from backing out though. I was trapped in hell, and there was no way out. I started to tremble noticeably.

"Relax," one of the captains told me. "If your opponent sees you scared, it will give him confidence."

"I'm too nervous," I whispered to him. "I've never done anything like this before." The butterflies in my stomach must have had talons on their bodies. I hurt terribly.

"Hey, I felt the same way my first varsity match," he consoled.

"Did you win?" I asked hopefully.

"No. I got pinned in eight seconds. I was never so embarrassed in my life."

I was called to the mat right then. I could already feel myself being thrown through the air helplessly and slammed mercilessly to the mat. I needed to go to the bathroom badly. I became consumed with the helpless feelings I had known when Dad had thrown me against the wall. I was sure there could be no fun in this.

While shaking hands with my opponent, I looked him over carefully. I hoped to see some kind of weakness, but nothing was apparent. He was three or four inches taller than I was and looked to weigh at least twenty pounds more.

The ref blew the whistle and yelled, "Wrestle."

The kid attacked me and had me on my back in an instant. I heard the moans from my teammates. I couldn't let it end that quickly. I kicked my legs hard and rolled. As I got on top of him, I locked my arms around his head, neck, and one arm. I squeezed as hard as I could. I heard things popping in his neck as he grunted in pain. I thought I might be hurting him, but I was too scared to let up. I just kept squeezing with all my strength.

"Pinned," the ref called out as he slapped the mat.

I was stunned and still didn't let go.

"You can let him go now, son," the ref assured me. "The match is over."

I was frozen and couldn't release my grip. I heard the boy beneath me sobbing. I was dazed and couldn't unravel the confusion in my mind.

"Let him go," one of the team captains laughed as he pried my hands loose. "You won the match. It's over."

He lifted me up, and the ref held up my arm to declare me the winner. The cheers from the crowd brought tears to my eyes. *Why would people cheer a bad person?* Just because I won a wrestling match didn't make me anything other than what I was. Maybe they didn't know me. I was glad. It felt good to win.

The longer I wrestled that year the more I realized that our coach wasn't a wrestling coach except by title. He had never wrestled and was in that position only because no one else would do it. He taught English. Our practices were run by the two team captains. They were both very good wrestlers and did a lot to help me learn. By the end of the year, I had won seven matches all by pin and had lost four all by pin. I decided that I would do whatever it took to place high enough in district the next year to be able to go to state.

During the spring, we had a few weeks of wrestling in PE. At the end of our learning period, people were allowed to challenge anyone they wanted to wrestle. If the challenged wanted to accept, then they got extra points toward their grade. I didn't need any extra points since I already had an A coming, so I just enjoyed watching the matches. On the last day of challenges, I heard my name called. I looked up to see the grubby farm boy who had wanted to fight me on a number of occasions, pointing at me. I remembered his cow pie boots and dirty clothes. I thought he probably would smell like he looked.

The coach was laughing at the boy, "You're twenty pounds heavier than he is. That's not a fair match unless he wants to wrestle you."

I was delighted at the opportunity. This would give me a chance to work him over without having to beat him up. I quickly consented to the match. When I got near him, I realized my fear that he would smell like he looked. He smelled just like a barn.

When we started to wrestle, I faked up and dove a single leg takedown. I pulled hard on the leg and sent him to the floor with a lot of force. He banged noisily. When he started to sit up, I quickly put a scissor-lock around his stomach and tightened it. This was an illegal hold in wrestling, but I figured the coach wouldn't know and I knew how much I could hurt this boy with the hold. He fought hard to get free, but the more he fought, the harder I squeezed. It didn't take long before he was unable to gasp a full breath. He was panting, trying to suck in the air his body was demanding.

"Make him stop," he moaned to the coach.

The coach had a big grin on his face and told him that I had to pin him or he had to say he gave up.

"I won't give up," he gasped.

My grip got tighter, and his face changed from red to white, then purple. He wasn't fighting anymore and looked slimy and sick. Sweat rolled off his face in small streamlets. Finally, he whispered that he gave up. Some of the bigger boys in the class who disliked me had told me they were going to challenge me also, but that match must have scared them off. At the end of the semester when I got my report card, I had a C in PE.

I always worked hard in PE and knew that I deserved an A even without being on the wrestling team. I asked my Mom to go talk to the coach about lying to me. I didn't get As very often, and I had earned this one.

"Oh, just ignore it. It doesn't matter," she shunned my pleas for justice.

# 17

*For those of you who can't take a.....joke.*

—Billy Connolly

"What did you two do?" the shop teacher asked my friend and me. "The principal wants to see you, and he's not happy. You better get over there quick."

We looked at each other in real bewilderment. We assured the shop teacher that we had done nothing to justify Snort being angry with us. On the way to his office, we discussed and wondered but could think of nothing we had done to warrant a visit with the pig.

"Get in here and sit down," Snort ordered us. We went into his inner office where students go only when in trouble. He slammed the door behind him to put emphasis on his displeasure with us. I was already too scared for that to add to my discomfort. I looked at my friend and could see by the white sheen covering his face that he must be just as worried as I was. The board of Education was hanging on the wall directly across from us. Looking at it mixed a small twinge of anger into my jangled emotions. I wondered if he had brought us in here planning to use that. I wasn't too sure if I would stand for that. Respect for adults or not, I didn't think I would just hold still for a whipping with that board.

"Well, gentlemen, *or should I call you worms?*" he fumed dramatically.

I almost laughed. My friend next to me snickered a little.

"So you think you're in here for fun and games, huh?" he addressed my friend. "I am not happy with you two," he bellowed as he struck my friend in the chest with the middle knuckle of his index finger. The hollow thump rang in my ears, and I started to heat with anger.

I decided that if he laid one finger on me, I would punch him and run out. I looked at the window of his office. Maybe I could jump out of it.

My friend and I looked at each other baffled. I began to wonder if we could get in trouble just because a teacher or the principal didn't like us. Maybe that was it.

"Don't you hit me again, or I'll hit you back," my friend finally gurgled out.

This shocked me. He wasn't usually that aggressive. He was a prankster with other students, but neither of us were disrespectful to teachers.

"Just because my Mom died doesn't mean you can pick on me. What the heck did we do?" he demanded.

This outburst surprised the principal. He surely wasn't used to being sassed. It didn't take him long to recompose though.

"You see that paddle on the wall?" he asked. "I'm probably going to use it on you two. I'm going to let you think about what you've done for a while and then come back, and I want you to tell me about it."

He left us for about ten minutes, but we didn't have a clue as to why we were there. He then reentered the room.

"Well, have you decided to tell me what you did?" he squealed.

"We don't have any idea what you're talking about," we both spoke at once.

Snort looked at us with a pondering stare.

"I'm going to let you go back to class. You think about this but do not talk to anyone about it. I mean absolutely do not discuss this with a single soul. Do you understand me?"

"Yes," we assured him.

"All right, go and think about it and come back here at the beginning of the next period," he snorted at us or, as my friend put it, "oinked" at us.

In class, a number of guys wanted to know what had happened. We told them and said we had no idea what it was about. We spent the rest of class time wondering what we had done. Just as the bell rang, my friend jumped up.

"I know what it is!" he shouted excitedly.

"What?" I asked.

"That girl in health class. The one I told the Almond Joy joke to."

"No way," I told him. "That's totally stupid. That was weeks ago, and no one would cause trouble over that."

"I know where her locker is," he said excitedly. "Let's get there quick." He headed out the door before I could say a thing.

When we got to her locker, she was there crying.

"What's wrong with you?" my friend demanded.

"Nothing, mind your own business," she sobbed.

"I know you lied about us, didn't you?" he persisted. "That's why Snort is after us. You tell me right now. You're not leaving here till I know."

"Yes," she sobbed harder.

"You know I just told a stupid joke. What did you tell Snort?" he grilled her more. By this time, they were attracting a crowd, and she was crying out of control.

"Leave me alone," she screamed.

"Come on," I urged him. "Let's go talk to Snort. Play like we don't know anything, okay," I suggested, fearing Snort would paddle us for sure if he knew we had talked to the girl.

I hated going into his office with kids still in the hall. They would see us, and there would be all kinds of rumors running rampant around the school.

"Sit down!" Snort ordered as we entered his office. His face was red and very angry looking.

"Do you remember what you did now?" he squealed in a high voice.

"Yeah, we know," my friend snapped at him. "We talked to a girl from our health class, and she was crying."

"I told you not to discuss this outside this office!" Snort steamed hotter than ever. "I just got back from talking to the girls' PE teacher and she, the girl, and I are very upset with you two."

"In the first place, he didn't have anything to do with it," my friend said pointing at me. "And in the second place, whatever she told you was a lie. All I did was tell her a joke."

I was sure Snort was going to explode. His ears were dark red and perked up high. I thought I could even see red-hot skin through his thick hair. He grabbed his paddle and waved it at my friend.

"Watch your mouth or I will use this on you!" he threatened. "You've really upset that girl and hurt her reputation."

"All I did was ask her what was six inches long and had two nuts and told her it was an Almond Joy," he answered hurriedly before Snort could cut him off.

I nodded in agreement.

Snort was silent for a moment, then seemed to steam again. I guessed he didn't like anyone bucking his authority. He turned beat red once more, and his pudgy face enlarged.

"She said you were telling kids that she was pregnant. Why would she say that?" he demanded. "That is a vicious rumor to tell about someone."

"Well, she is a liar, and we didn't say anything like that," my friend snapped back.

"You two get out of my office, and if anything happens like this again, you will be expelled," he yelled at us.

"I'd like to thump knots on his head," my friend said as we headed back to class. "What a fat jerk! And that stupid, idiot girl. I'm going to kick her butt."

I warned him that we would be way better off if he would just drop it. The incident didn't drop though. We both got tons of cold stares and crude remarks thrown at us for quite some time.

My friend and I wondered and discussed at length what the heck was wrong with girls. They had to be the strangest creatures on earth.

Toward the end of the ninth grade, another incident set me in the muck at school. In PE, we were to always put our towels into the laundry basket. Coach was constantly telling us that he was not our mother and no way would he pick up after us. My friend and I had no problem with this because we had a contest each day rolling up our towels and shooting them into the basket. We kept a running total score over a month's time to see who could score the most. On one particular day I made it and he missed. He picked his towel up and slam dunked it into the basket. The area we dressed in was now empty except for a towel on the floor. At least eight of us had dressed in that area. Coach walked in just as someone yelled for whoever left their towel to pick it up.

"I'll get it," my friend volunteered.

"I saw you put yours in the basket," someone told him.

"You leave it there," the coach huffed. "Whose towel is that?" he bellowed.

No one was willing to sacrifice themselves to his anger, but one boy hollered my name as a suspect.

"He shot his into the basket," my friend stuck up for me.

"Sure, he's your buddy. It figures you'd stick up for him," the dirty farm boy, whom I had wrestled, accused.

"I put mine in there," I said threateningly. I was greatly angered at the attention being focused on me. "There were more than just us two over there."

Coach held our class over till we were late for our next one.

"All of you meet me in the library at noon," he ordered.

We spent the entire lunch hour listening to a lecture on cleanliness. Then we were told we'd be there every day until the guilty one fessed up. I doubted anyone would because this coach was mean. He had hurt kids hitting them with shoes and towels and got a big kick from it. Besides, I doubted that whoever left the towel would remember anyway.

After the third lunch hour in the library, kids began accusing one another. Girls got involved in it too. I probably got the most persecution from it. Some guys would shove me as I passed them in the halls. Girls would call me chicken, baby, and some worse names. The grubby farm kid seemed to be on a campaign to make my life miserable. On the fourth day, we got a big lecture about cowards and making others suffer because we weren't man enough to face up to our own responsibilities. I had been napping when I heard my name. I looked up, and the sunlight reflected off a window into my eyes causing them to water and blur. I wiped away the watery fuzz and saw the farm boy staring at me.

"Why you cryin'?" he mused. "You must be guilty."

"Shut your stupid face or I will after school," I warned him.

He turned away. After school, a group of girls, led by the big mouth I had met my first day at Harden, confronted me.

"Why don't you just admit you did it and let everyone else off the hook?" the big mouth blurted.

"Because it wasn't mine," I told her. "If it had been mine, I'm probably the only one not too chicken to admit it."

"Why were you crying today then?" she asked.

"I wasn't crying," I told her. "My eyes were watering like they do all the time."

"Yeah, I bet. You stinkin' baby. All our boyfriends are missing lunches because of you. If you had any guts, you'd confess even if you didn't do it."

"Well, I didn't do it, and I won't confess to protect a bunch of cowards," I sneered at her.

The next day, the lunchtime punishments were cancelled because too many parents had complained to Snort. That didn't help my cause though. It seemed all the rock walls were being piled up again. Even my friend hung around me less. I was shut out of group gatherings again, and vicious stares from boys and girls became commonplace. I was glad school was close to an end for that year. On the last day, we had an afternoon dance. The girl I liked was standing across the floor looking at me, and I motioned toward the dance floor. She shook her head no and turned her back to me. I could see the prison doors slamming in my face and heard that lonely echo through my heart and mind. I went home very sad.

## 18

*Work keeps us from three great evils: boredom, vice, and need.*

—Voltaire

The summer between my freshman and sophomore years just flew by. My brothers and I had reputations as hard and good workers, so farmers were always calling us. I didn't have much free time to worry about anything but work. For that, I was grateful. Many times during the summer I was attacked with pangs of loneliness and hopelessness. I missed the companionship of the only person whom I counted as a true friend. Working hard often helped me to cope with such bad feelings. Each time I would see that girl though, those feelings would well up and overshadow my indifference to life. This would drive me to work harder, to push myself to physical extremes killing the pangs of loneliness with terrible aches and pains.

When school resumed, I started where I had left off—no friends and everyone seemingly mad at me. At football practice, I was a running back/receiver. Regardless of whether the play was called to me or not, I never got the ball. The bigger defensive guys were always cheap-shotting me, and the coaches seemed amused by it all. I quit the team and worked on my own to prepare for wrestling. I decided my whole year would revolve around wrestling and track. I worked desperately to be prepared to go to state, and I was confident I could make it.

When wrestling finally started, the team was quite different from the previous year. The two captains, who had helped me so much, were gone, most of the varsity was changed, and a couple of our better wrestlers had moved away. The two new captains were hostile toward me from the beginning. I was a 105-pounder, and they were both five or six weight classes up. They worked to make life miserable for me. Since they basically ran the team, they were frequently making me do extra running and pushups along with wrestling guys much bigger than me. They all did things to try to injure me. Once in a while, the coach would interfere. Toward the end of the season, I injured my shoulder wrestling a guy who weighed 180 pounds. Because of this, the coach finally put limits on whom they could make me wrestle. I wrestled every varsity match at my weight that year. I had a good win-loss record. I never had any challenges to my varsity spot because I could easily pin all the other 105 pounders. In the district seedings, I was in the bottom bracket, which gave me a good chance to get to state. I had beat all but one of the wrestlers in that bracket and had barely lost to him. I just needed to win my first two matches to guarantee going to the state tournament.

A few days before districts, we had our final challenges for the varsity spots. The coach told me my spot was closed because I was the only one who had wrestled varsity all year. During my wrestle off, he wanted me to work for a while instead of just pinning my opponent quickly. The number 2 105-pounder was my age and good friends with the team captains. They went to church together, and their families were close acquaintances. I had no worry of my spot though because I had never lost to this particular boy, and I knew I could pin him easily.

On challenges night he came up and asked me to not pin him too quickly so he wouldn't be real embarrassed.

"I know you'll win," he said. "So just use me for practice."

The coach also asked me again to get some exercise and not just pin him quickly.

As we wrestled, I practiced some new moves I had been working on during the year but not in matches. I was concentrating hard not paying attention to the score. I was doing virtually whatever I wanted to with him. At the end of round 2, the captains said he was ahead 8–3. One of them was doing refereeing, and the other was keeping score. I became extremely angry knowing what they were trying to pull. I had no ill feelings toward my opponent. He was a quiet, friendly, and well-liked kid at school. No matter though I would do what it took to win the match. When the round started off, I immediately rolled him with a half nelson, my favorite move. As I turned him, I shoved his shoulder hard toward his head to let him know I wasn't clowning around anymore. I had him pinned in under ten seconds. I held his back flush to the mat for at least fifteen seconds and there was no call from the ref, so I squeezed him tighter to the point that I could tell it was hurting his neck. I finally squeezed him so hard that he screamed for them to stop the match. The captains took him aside for a short talk and then said the match was to continue.

"The match is over," I complained. "He gave up, and that ends it."

"You shut up and wrestle or forfeit," they warned me.

I was really ticked off and when they didn't even give me my near pin points, I felt rage surging through me. We started with me on top again. I let him up, which gave him a point, but I took him down quickly with a headlock and squeezed hard enough to pop his head off. I decided I would make him hurt so badly that he wouldn't want to continue. He gasped for air and squeaked for them to stop the match again.

"I give up!" he yelled. "He has me pinned."

I held him pinned for three times the required time. We were separated, and again the captains told him he had to keep wrestling. They still hadn't given me points for the takedown or the near pin. By this time, the coach was getting fidgety as I looked at and told the captain to ref it fair. He told me to shut up or forfeit. Finally, the coach told them to be fair and give me whatever I earned this time. They told him to shut up and mind his own business.

"What are you going to do, kick us all off the team and take only him to districts?" one of them jeered at him. I was positive he would kick them off the team. Instead, he sat down and said nothing.

I was so angry that my body was shaking and revving, waiting to get my hands on my wimpy opponent. I was going to make him pay dearly. As the match started, I quickly rolled him over and pinned him with the half nelson again. This time, I forced his head into my armpit and bent his neck until it popped, and he screamed in pain. I wasn't awarded points, so I let him go and let him get to his stomach. I then put a chicken wing on him and drove with full force pushing the joint of his shoulder up and inward. Again, he screamed in pain as I turned him over and pinned him easily. He had tears pouring down his cheeks, and he groaned his surrender. The captain stopped the match and declared him winner because he was supposedly ahead in points. I was baffled. My mind raced in savage confusion. My lips were numb and tingling, and I was gripped with a terrible chill. It all seemed to be a horrible dream. I looked around for help and support, but no one moved the slightest. The entire team was imprisoned in deathly silence. A dark hue closed in around the room, and it seemed no one even breathed. The coach finally got up and walked away. The boy I had beaten was lying near the wall, sobbing and rubbing his sore neck, and the team captains stared at me through dark, dark threatening eyes.

That evening, I was sick and couldn't eat. I didn't tell my parents about what had happened because I knew they didn't care. It meant nothing to them. But I cared. I was so confused and worried. I agonized over what recourse I had. There had to be some way for me to obtain justice. I finally decided that I needed to go back the next night and beat the kid again.

At practice that afternoon, I began wrestling the phony winner as we were dressing down. I would take him down and pin him, let him up, take him down, and pin him, and let him up again. I did this repeatedly. The coach finally told him that if I pinned him that easily again I would be going to districts. I was relieved. I would finally get my justice. When the coach started the match, I grabbed the boy and pinned him within five or six seconds.

"Now do I get to go to districts?" I asked confidently.

"I'm sorry," he said staring at the floor. "There is nothing I can do about this."

An enormous weight slammed into my mind. I was shocked and sick in every part of my body. My head tightened, and my lips numbed. I wanted to cry, but I couldn't. I glared hatefully at the coach, and he left the room. I was so disgusted with him for being such a stinking coward. I hated the boy I had beaten for being so chicken as not to admit his defeat. But most of all, I hated the team captains. They were the biggest cowards I had ever known. I wondered how they could have any respect for themselves. *How could people treat me so cruelly and say I was so bad when I was surrounded by such awful beings?* Poison began filling my soul with a desire to bite the whole world with venomous fangs and watch it all decay and rot.

I wanted my parents to come to the school and intervene on my behalf, but I knew that they wouldn't. Mom insisted that it wasn't important and I should be man enough to ignore it. I thought of being such an outcast and became glad. I hated everyone and didn't want or need any friends.

At districts, my first match would have been against a kid I had beaten twice that year. Our guy lost to him by pin in the first round and was out of the tournament. I was glad, but I still hurt and was hateful to all the cowards who had robbed me of my rightful chance to go to state.

As it turned out, the points I would probably have won would have given our team the district championship. That didn't make me feel any better though.

Later that year, I earned a varsity letter in track by placing second in a major invitational. At the end of the season, the coaches didn't give me the letter. The hurt was minimal because I was becoming numb emotionally, but I wondered how that dark force around me could have such a negative effect on all who dealt with me. My brothers and sisters all had friends and were treated normal. *Why then was I so different? Why did everyone have to treat me like I was an enemy?* I thought of the dark shadow that had appeared at the end of my bed. I wondered if perhaps it followed me and had something to do with all this. *Why had it targeted me? Why did even the one person who could offer me a little bit of happiness reject me and refuse to even give me a charitable smile?* It had been so long since I had made that stupid, innocent mistake, and she still wouldn't talk to me even though she professed to care about me. This couldn't be normal. Something unseen had to be interfering with my daily life. That hurt and loneliness dug deep into my soul and sent shockwaves of pain to the very pit of my heart. Personal attacks at school had increased again, and I drifted alone through a sea of demons and frightened silent shadows.

## 19

*No alternative was presented but resistance, or
unconditional submission. Between these
could be no hesitation.*

—Thomas Jefferson

One lunch hour, I was walking down the hall, and a group of boys came by. One of them leaned over and bumped me with his shoulder. I wheeled around and hit him in the back of the head. When he turned, I grabbed him and threw him hard against the wall. I cursed him in language I hadn't used before and threatened to mutilate his face if he ever touched me again. One of his friends asked if I planned on fighting all of them. I turned and drove both of my fists into his chest sending him to the floor.

"Yes, I will if you ever bother me again," I promised between clenched teeth. The other boys were white and solemn-looking. They didn't say a word.

When I turned and walked away, the silence of the crowded hall ripped through me. I hurt and hated and wondered again, *Why me?*

That year ended with one more fight. I was watching some kids playing football at noon, and one very big kid was being rough with the smaller ones. He threw one of my brothers down, and I headed after him. The closer I got, the bigger he became. When I was next him, I couldn't see over or around his broad shoulders.

"You lay off the little kids," I said to him, adding some cuss words, which were now becoming a habit with me.

"I'm not afraid of you, you—" he swore back.

I hit him in the mouth hard and quick. Blood began to flow.

"I'm not going to fight you," he said coldly. "But I'm not afraid of you."

The next day at noon, he sent someone into the school to get me. When I got close, he pushed me. I wrestled him to the ground and squeezed his neck in a headlock until he started gasping for air. He said he had had enough. The following day, he sent for me again.

"Today I'll fight," he boasted proudly.

"Good for you," I said sarcastically. "Let's not waste time."

As he came close, I pushed him back, then pushed him again and kept pushing him till he was against the school.

"Why don't you push me back?" I said cursing at him.

"I will when I'm ready. Don't worry," he promised.

He stepped toward me, and I hit him hard in the mouth. He started bleeding again from his nose. His eyes filled with tears, and he dropped his hands.

"You stupid baby," I said disgustedly. "Don't pick on little kids anymore." And then I walked away.

## 20

*I wanna be a high school football hero,*
*With an S.A.T. score less than zero.*

—Davey Havok

The new summer was busier than the previous ones. Before it began, we had work lined up for most of the three months we had off. The work was hot and dirty, but for some sadistic reason, I loved it. My mind was occupied with being able to work harder and faster than anyone else. By doing this, I was always too tired to worry about school, the kids around, or anything else.

Many of the parents at church didn't like our family (at least us boys) and often made snide remarks to us about what kind of kids we were. Scouting was incorporated into a church program. My brothers and I loved this part of church and did much toward earning Eagle awards. When it came time for our advancements though, they wouldn't give them to us because, as they put it, we weren't worthy of it. This was a great distress to my older brother. He had put a lot of work into getting his Eagle. He would have been the first in this troop in over twenty years. When he was denied the award, he was deeply hurt. He pleaded with Mom and Dad to go do something. One day, he was talking to Mom about it, and I heard her tell him to just ignore it. I was getting good at just ignoring some things, so not getting my advancements didn't bother me as much.

The new school year was one which I was apprehensive about. Something was different inside me. With all the injustices I had become used to previously, I had some sense of forgiving. I had felt somehow responsible for the way others treated me. It was a submissive, I deserve it, feeling. Now, I was bitter. I had built up an intense hatred and resentment toward anyone who looked at me in the wrong way. I had an almost overpowering urge to beat up most people around me. It became a constant struggle to refrain from fighting all the time. I didn't like being mistreated and wanted to fight back to put an end to the slightest hint of abuse. Being at school every day, around so many jerks, would just make my life more miserable.

On the first day of football practice, a group of boys had called and said they would pick me up. I lived on their way to the school. I was ready and somewhat anxious to play this year. I wanted to release a bunch of pent up energy and anger. I still wasn't very big (about five feet, four inches tall and a hundred and twenty pounds). With the work ethic I had built, I was sure I could make up for my lack in size. I was ready and excited when it came time for them to pick me up.

At the appointed time, they went speeding by our house, honking and waving. I hated them so badly. I swore and went back into the house. I started thinking of how I would get each one of them alone and kick the daylights out of them. The following day at practice, one of them loudly informed me that they had forgotten all about me the day before. They all had a good laugh over it. During practice, I was a total reject. No one on the team would talk to me. Only the coaches spoke to me. The other players wouldn't even look at me. It went this way for the first week and a half. One evening, we were doing tackling drills against the running backs. On my first turn, the biggest back on the team came up. I was sure this was by design. He weighed over two hundred pounds. I didn't care about the size difference. I hated him as much as I hated most of the team and wanted to hit him hard enough to hurt him. When the whistle blew, my hate and anger threw me at him with all my force. I hit his huge thigh and heard a pop as a lightning bolt of pain shot through my shoulder and head. My right arm went limp, but I kept grabbing with my left hand as I saw his feet move by. I caught one of his socks and tripped him to the ground.

"That's exactly what we want," one of the coaches yelled delightedly. "We want all of you to go after your tackles just like that." He complimented me on a great job as he slapped my helmet.

By the time I reached the back of the line, some of my fingers were numb, and my right hand and arm were stinging with sharp, needle-like pains. It was excruciating, and I had to fight not to show the torment. As I neared the front of the line, I saw the backs jockeying around so I would have the same back again. My anger flared up and erupted enough to deaden the pain as I again hit him with every ounce of hatred I could summon. We collided, and the pain in my right shoulder seared through my head, neck, and back. I bounced off him as before but was determined not to let him get by me. With my right hand, I caught an ankle and wrapped my finger around it. He fell forward and jerked pulling my hurt shoulder. The pain turned into a scorching fire consuming my whole upper torso. I fought hard not to scream out as weakness raced through my body. Again, the coach raved about what a great effort that was and if our whole team were that determined, we wouldn't lose a game all year. A few of the guys patted my helmet and complimented me, but I was in too much pain to care. When I got to the back of the line, I found that I couldn't move my right arm. It hung limp and wouldn't respond to any of my efforts to raise it. I couldn't quit. I was sure everyone would think I was a sissy if I quit now.

"Man, what's wrong with your arm?" the boy in front of me gasped. His eyes were wide and wild-looking.

"Nothing," I told him as I tried to lift it and show it was okay. A new surge of pain forced a groan between my gritted teeth.

"Hey, Coach," he yelled urgently to the nearest one. "Come look at this guy's arm."

"What did you do?" he growled at me.

"He didn't do anything," the boy interrupted. "But look at his right arm. He can't even move it."

The coach looked at me and told me to take off my pads. The boy watching gagged and let out a long moan as he saw my shoulder. There was a large lump under my skin where a bone was elevated about two inches. Some other boys around gasped as they saw it.

"You better go get dressed, and I'll get you to the doc," he ordered. He sent the manager to call my parents.

At the doctor's office, my arm was put in a sling, and I was told to keep it there for two weeks. That meant I'd have to wear the sling to school. I was petrified at the thought of wearing it in public. There was no way I could handle the attention it would draw. I could bear the physical pain much easier than the mental anguish that would cause.

The next morning when I showed up at breakfast without the sling, Mom insisted that I put it on. I protested violently, but she wouldn't give in. As I left the house to get on the bus, I took it off. Each morning, I repeated this when I was away from her. Two weeks later, there was still a big lump on top of the shoulder. It looked like a big bony knob. Mom sent me to a different doctor, and he said it was dislocated. He put me in a chair and held me in an awkward position and jerked hard. There was a new blast of pain, and I felt something pop. The lump was gone. He taped it very tightly and told me not to move my arm at all or it wouldn't stay in. He said I had waited too long to be seen, and if it didn't stay in, it would take surgery to keep it in place. Driving home, I turned the steering wheel to go around a corner, and my shoulder popped out again. I told Mom what the doctor had said, and she told me to ignore it.

## 21

*Men have less compunction about harming*
*someone who had made himself loved than*
*harming someone who has made himself feared.*

—Niccolo Machiavelli

At the beginning of this new school year, I was treated like a fresh cow plop. People around our area were familiar with those and were always careful to step around them. At first, I was amused. It was so obvious that it must be a game. As time passed though, I became angrier about it. My mind started racing with unanswerable questions as to why I was such a freak. Absolutely no one would talk to me. Even teachers didn't look at me when they gave me my papers. *What dark shadow was casting this horrible spell? I hadn't done anything I could understand to deserve such abuse.* I became harder and more bitter inside. The hardness was sheer hatred, and the bitterness was spite for those around me, including my family. I was embarrassed to be treated that way, and I felt that my family had to be partly responsible even though they weren't treated as I was. The cold environment fired up my emotions and tossed them into icy, jagged confusion. At one point during the year, I weakened and begged my brothers to hang around with me during lunch because I felt so outcast. But even they couldn't break through that stony barrier into my world. It embarrassed them to be seen with me. There was no explicable reason for my mystical treatment. There was just some dark influence that persisted around my world, and it was beyond my comprehension.

Soon, I began to daydream frequently and for long periods. My fantasies would carry over from one class to the next. This kept me partially protected from the glares and whispers as I existed at school. During some classes, I would count the letter *O* in opposite columns of my books and count each line as a particular weight class in wrestling. The number of *O*s would represent the score of the match, and thus I could have team competitions in my fantasy world. This was fun and helped time pass more quickly and less painfully. Other times, I would watch the clock and time 15, 30, 45, and 60 seconds. I would draw *O*s as fast as I could in each time and see what records I could set and break doing this activity. Each record I set was a world record and helped me feel a little important because I was the world champion at something. When these became too boring, I loved to daydream about being in the mountains. I adored the beauty of the streams flowing crisply along through snow-white surroundings. The crystal clear ice crusts built along the edges of the creek and the frosted trees lining the banks spreading into a vast wilderness of privacy and wonder excited me. The mountains were magnificent, peaceful, and unstained by human filth and rudeness. I daydreamed of the many nights I would walk alone in the chilling cold with huge snowflakes floating slowly to the ground, landing softly on my cheeks and nose and melting into frozen icelets on my face.

As hard and bitter as I was becoming, I often cried myself to sleep. I would lay in bed thinking of wanting to talk to that special someone and get that sad, empty yearning for companionship. It would build and fill my soul with despair and aloneness. *How could I be among so many people and not have a soul to share a few moments and feelings with?* I would fight hard not to think of it, tried to ignore it all, but my throat would squeeze tight, and tears would involuntarily flood my eyes. The warmness of the streams crawling down my face kept reminding me of the cold loneliness I felt within. The cold, wet stains left on my pillow taught how out of place I was. I hated it all. I shouldn't be such a baby. I wanted to be more adult about it and learn to ignore everything. As the year wore on, I became stronger. The lonely feelings became much easier to squash and overcome. I got tougher, harder, and more serious. I didn't feel the need to bluff anymore. I wanted those who dared trespass on my feelings to know they would be prosecuted severely.

One afternoon, I was on the bus to go home. I had an arm bent with my elbow out the window. One of my brother's friends jumped up and grabbed my elbow. His weight jerked my arm down and sent a bolt of pain through my armpit. He quickly apologized, but the pain had sent my emotions to eruption level. I flew off the bus in a rage. I liked this kid. He was very quiet and friendly with most people. But he had trespassed. He had to be punished for his crime against me. By the time I got off the bus, a small crowd had already gathered. My brothers asked me to drop it because this kid was a very good friend. He was also smaller than I was. I wanted to back away and let it go, but I couldn't. He had to pay. Everyone had to know that if they hurt me, they would suffer too. The grubby farm boy was there, sneering at me about picking on someone smaller than I was. I told him he'd be next. Kids were thick around us. Their faces looked like imps of the underworld yearning for some evil adventure. Eyes were wide, and people were screaming for him to hit me. I hated being here. I could feel the devilish shadows lurking around and see them in many faces. While I was digesting this scene and hating being the center of attention, the boy reached up and hit me. A hard thud echoed through my head. My ears rang, and blackness closed my vision. Darting flashes of light were all I could see. My face stung where he had landed the punch. I started swinging hard and blindly in the direction I had known he was in. I heard clearly the screaming, cheering, and prodding as my blows landed. I let my instincts lead me through a still darkened world. I worried that my sight would never return. After a few solid hits, he fell to the ground still and quiet. I tripped over him, and the unkind hands caught me and shoved me back to my feet. As my vision slowly returned, more hands were shoving me from all directions. Taunts were filtering through my head from the hostile group. Others were bent over my fallen foe with stunned looks on their faces. I pushed my way through the crowd and got back onto the bus. Justice had been served. I could feel good about that.

The next day, I missed school. I didn't want to see anyone, and I wanted no one to see me. Too many kids had seen that fight, too much would be made of it. I didn't want to walk the gauntlet of stares through the halls. After school, the boy I had fought came home with my brothers and apologized. He smiled and revealed a big, empty space between two teeth.

"You sure hit hard," he said in mock compliment. "I've never been hit like that before. I'll never get you mad at me again."

## 22

*The essence of war is violence.*
*Moderation in war is imbecility.*

—Sea Lord John Fisher

When wrestling started, I was grateful and excited. It would give
me a chance to work off some of my aggressiveness legitimately.
At the first practice, I dressed quickly and was the first one
running the halls. I ran hard to feel all my muscles swell and burn
energy. I needed to work to oblivion. As I rounded a corner, I
nearly ran into some kid I didn't know. He was a big kid though.
When I circled back, he pushed me into the wall as we passed.
A storm clouded my head with violent emotion, and my muscles
throbbed with new volcanic bursts. I ran harder as a new flow
of energy filled my veins. I was anxious to get back to where he
was. When I turned the corner into his hall, he got into my path,
and we were headed stubbornly toward each other. He flipped
me the finger, I slowed, with my fist doubled as I neared him.
Within a few yards of him, I lunged forward and drove my fist
with a hard shot to his face. I heard him bang noisily against the
lockers, and I turned to see him sitting on the floor. His friends
were there quickly to help him up. I slowed, coming back to see
if he wanted to pursue his challenge, but he declined. By the time
we had all gathered to the auditorium stage for practice, his eye
was blackened and swollen. Our new coach looked at him, then

at me, and back to him. I didn't know this coach, but he didn't look very happy right then.

"What happened to you?" he questioned.

"I ran into a door," he answered coolly.

The coach looked at me as if he were going to say something. He was very angry. Then he turned away and started practice.

I worked hard during wrestling. Whomever I wrestled got the worst that I could deal out. I still felt extremely isolated even around my fellow wrestlers, and I let those feelings transform into valuable energy. I didn't smile as much as I had used to. Hate and anger were now the rulers of my life in all situations. Many of the wrestlers on our team hated to wrestle against me and often refused. I didn't care how anyone felt though. I was determined that what had happened the previous year wouldn't have a chance to happen again.

By district time, I had done well enough to have a shot at state again. My weight class was a tough one that year though. Many wrestlers had started losing excess weight to get down two or three weight classes. This made it so that I was wrestling guys who looked like they were twice my size. I had done well enough to get a decent seed, and with the right breaks, I knew I could make it to state. All I needed to do was to win two matches in a row, and I would go for sure. My first match would be a breeze, but the second was with one of the weight jumpers. He had needed to lose over fifteen pounds when we wrestled his school and hadn't made it for our match. He only lost one of the matches during the year in which he had made the weight. I figured if I wrestled hard, I could wear him out and beat him at the end.

A week and a half before districts, I was challenged for one last time by a tall, stout kid. He had wrestled a few matches of varsity in the weight above me and one at my weight because I had missed a practice and was punished for it. He was an aggressive wrestler, especially against me. This may have been due to the fact that he was one of the boys I had beat up in the seventh grade.

He was taller, broader, and looked much heavier than I. At the beginning of our match, I worked to build up points because he was one of those real flexible people who was hard to pin. Most of the team would rather have seen him go to district than me, but if he got it, he would definitely earn it. No one was going to win by cheating me this year. Our coach was too honest and was no coward-like the one the year before.

By the end of the second round, I was up 6–0. He was on top to start the third, and I decided to go for a pin real quick in that round. I stood up immediately on the whistle. My left heel stuck on the mat and tripped me. The momentum took us both down. His right leg was between my right shin and the mat. He fell full weight on the back of my ankle. My right toe stuck in the mat, forcing the bottom of my foot upward as his weight drove my leg down. I could feel popping and grinding in the ankle. A horrendous fire ignited like an explosion at the spot where he knelt on my leg, and it shot pain up the leg and throughout my body. I was swollen in anguish as I tried to suppress the scream, which forced its way through my clenched jaw. All strength left my limbs. I tried desperately to get up to tell the coach I would never quit this match no matter what, but each movement brought a lashing of pain and stomach sickness. I tried to claw my way to the edge of the mat. I needed desperately to reach the wall to get the support to get to my feet. Some of the wrestlers tried to help me.

"No," I insisted. "I'm not quitting this match. We're going to finish it."

My head was light and pounding. Streaks of lightning flashed thunderously through my ankle and leg. My body started shaking while drops of sweat mugged my face with more discomfort. Tears were fighting through my determination, pouring from the four corners of my eyes. Those around me were blurred, stony figures staring at me in silence. I wouldn't give any of them the satisfaction of seeing me down. I turned to my knees, then up on my left leg while digging my fingers into the wall for support.

"I'm not quitting," I insisted. "Let's finish the match."

I stepped lightly onto my right foot, and the thunder of pain slammed me back to the mat.

"Tape it," I begged. "Just get it taped tight so I can finish."

I rolled to my side and stared hard at the coach.

"Don't make me quit. I can finish."

His face was pale and undecided. He stared at me in hollow silence. The quiet of the room pounded through my scorching mind.

*They want to see me gone, just like last year*, I thought. *I'm not going to quit. I've earned it.*

I rolled to my knees again and back up on my left leg. Pain attacked cruelly again as my right foot touched the mat. I stayed up. I could go on and would go on.

"I'm ready," I insisted as I hobbled to the center of the mat and got to my hands and knees in the down position.

The coach nodded approval, and the whistle blew. The kid immediately grabbed my right ankle and twisted. I lunged in pain but rolled to my back and kicked him in the chest with my good leg. Anger exploded in my mind and body firing with hatred through my system.

"You stinkin' jerk," I heard my brother yell. "Just wrestle him. Don't try to hurt his ankle anymore, or I'll kick your butt."

Ignoring my brother, my opponent ran toward me. I tried to think of a way to win quickly. He was too confident, and all I needed was one good hold. A rushing noise in my head muffled the cheering and encouragements from our teammates. He was coming at me in a very slow motion, it seemed. Sweat sprayed from his hair as he jerked his head up and lunged at me. I wondered if my ankle would hold. I waited, for what seemed like an eternity, for him to get to me. When he reached out, I slid left and grabbed his left wrist. I drove up hard and hateful off my right foot. I hit his hip with my shoulder and jerked his left arm down. This drove his face into the mat. I quickly jumped across his body and pulled his arm behind him and forced it upward. He groaned in pain as the pressure increased on the shoulder. Blood was staining the mat beneath his nose. I hit behind his head with a forearm and drove his face into the blood. He lashed out wildly from the pain and anger and kicked my sore ankle. Involuntarily, I released his wrist and rolled to my back in horrid agony. Chills blanketed my body, and even my teeth began to hurt. I wondered how I could possibly finish the match. My body had turned cruelly against me shutting off the strength my hatred had fueled. Even my desire was dampened by the awful weakness that flooded over me.

"That's enough," the coach ordered as he came to help me.

"No," I begged. "I can finish. Please don't make me quit."

My stomach churned with nausea. I would fight for all I was worth for this win. If I could just get a small reprieve from the pain, I could continue. Anger boiled inside me again. If this boy took my place at districts, I'd catch him at school and beat him half to death.

"We'll wait until tomorrow to decide about this," the coach promised.

I didn't like what I sensed in his voice. It was saying he was postponing the inevitable. I was relieved though. At least I would have a chance to prove that I could make it. I laid back and wallowed in my pain. I was surprised and wondered why the coach would give me that second chance.

I fell asleep that night trying to figure how to win the match the next day. He would certainly work my ankle so I plotted moves to counter whatever he might try. I needed to be able to get him into a quick pinning hold. The longer the match went, the better his chances would be.

I slept very little that night. Every movement I made sent thrusts of pain through the ankle and leg. By morning, I was exhausted.

At practice, the coach told me not to dress down. I was furious. The other boy was already dressed down.

"But I'm okay," I insisted. "I can wrestle him now."

"I believe you." He smiled. "We'll just wait."

"You're not going to push me out of districts, are you?"

"We'll just wait and see. Right now, I'm not going to let you make that ankle worse. If you do, you won't go for sure. Did you see the doctor last night?" he added.

"No, my Mom doesn't believe much in doctors."

If I had told Mom how bad it hurt, she would have told me to ignore it.

Coach didn't let me practice at all till two days before districts. He had met with the team captains, and they had decided I was going. This was a tremendous surprise to me. I wondered why people who didn't like me would do anything nice for me. I was happy and relieved.

The day of districts, my foot was taped very tightly. I could barely put any pressure on it, and the pain was constant and throbbing. The first time I stepped down on the foot, a knifing stab sliced up the inside of my leg and to my thigh, and I fell to the ground. I quickly got up and tried to act as if the fall was a slip. The coach looked at me and shook his head.

"I don't know about this," he said. "Maybe I better reconsider."

"I'm fine," I promised. "I think the tape is just too tight."

After re-taping, I could hobble on it a little better.

My first match was as I had assumed it would be. The kid made a feeble dive for my bad leg, and I dropped on him and pinned him quickly with a half nelson. Before my second match, my opponent came to visit me.

"My coach says your leg is so bad that you shouldn't be allowed to wrestle, is that right?"

"No," I answered calmly. "I wrestled on it the day I hurt it. It's fine."

"Well, I figured you'd be between me and state this year, and I'll do whatever it takes to get there. I just thought I'd warn you before our match."

"Good for you," I replied as he walked away.

Our match was a standoff for the first two rounds. He led 3–2 to start the third, but I was in the down position, which I always felt was to my advantage. I could work better from there, and it was easier to score quickly from the bottom. At the beginning of the round, each time I was close to an escape or reversal, he would just drive me out of bounds. This was supposed to be stalling, but the ref wasn't calling it. This gave him a big advantage. I started working harder and moving quicker, which got him breathing hard. Just over halfway through the round, I knew I had him. He was gasping to breathe, and I could feel his arms weakening. He had just pushed me out of bounds, and I decided I would go for a quick standup reverse when the ref started us. The whistle blew, and I brought my left foot and knee up immediately. I started to stand, and he drove his knee onto the back of my right ankle. The flickering pain, which had been there all day ignited brutally and forced me to sprawl on the mat. I was determined to fight through his cheap shot, but before I could recover, he had grabbed the hurt ankle and used it as a lever to turn me to my back. As I was bridging, I could hear his coach yelling for him to drive me toward my hurt side. I spent the remainder of the round bridging off my right leg trying to avoid the pin.

"I knew I'd beat you on that ankle," he bragged as we shook hands.

I hobbled off the mat having lost my chance at state. For me to still go, he would have to win his next match and allow me to remain in the tournament. It was very unlikely that he could beat the guy he was matched with, and he didn't.

## 23

*I daresay that in the spirit world,*
*when it was proposed*
*to us to come into this probation, and pass*
*through the experience*
*that we are now receiving, it was not altogether pleasant*
*and agreeable.*

—Lorenzo Snow

School went downhill after that. A boy a year younger than I got upset because I bumped him in the hall, and he dropped his books. I was hurrying to class and just went on my way. During lunch, he came after me. I was outside watching kids playing on the football field when someone pushed me from behind.

"Hey you…" he swore at me. "Why'd you knock my books on the floor?"

"I guess it's because you're so ugly, dork," I responded. "It was just an accident," I added as I turned away.

"Oh, bull," he screamed and shoved me again.

My whole body tightened with rage. When I turned to face him, I could see fear more than anything in his eyes. He was probably five inches taller than I was and at least thirty pounds heavier. He had dark-red hair and freckles. He was built like the other hardworking farm boys around there. I was aware that he had an older brother who was much bigger than him. I'd seen his brother fight before but not this kid.

"Have you ever been in a fight?" I asked him.

"What difference does that make?" he shot back.

"It hurts to get your face beat in," I said. "It doesn't bother me to get hit, but how are you going to feel when I kick your behind with all these kids around watching?" I asked coolly.

"I'm not afraid of you," he insisted. "I fight with my brother, and he's way bigger than you."

"So, I'm not afraid to fight your brother either," I said confidently. "Besides, I can probably whip him, but I know you can't."

He started shaking, and his eyes filled with tears. By now, a crowd had gathered along with one of my brothers.

"Don't be such a crybaby," my brother teased him. "He won't hurt you too bad."

"You shut your mouth," he snapped at my brother as he kicked at him.

This increased my anger, and I hit him. Immediately, his lip swelled and blood trickled down his chin. I hit him again in the chest, which sent him backward into the ground. Too many people were around, so I turned to leave.

"My brother will be looking for you," he bawled.

The next day, he was there again. I could see a more determined look in his eyes.

I pushed him backward once, then again, and a third time. Huge tears filled his eyes and magnified his freckles as they rolled over his face.

"Where's your big, tough brother?" I mocked him.

Suddenly, the crowd became very silent. I wondered what was going on. This must be a setup, and his brother was probably behind me ready to nail me.

I glanced behind me, then back at him. He started crying, and kids gathered around to console him. This was very weird.

"His brother was killed in a car wreck last night, you jerk," someone sneered at me.

I looked at my brother. "Why'd he come to school?" I asked blankly. "It figures that I'd turn out to be the bad guy even over something like this."

In school, I was scowled at worse than ever.

*Who sets me up for these things?* I wondered. *It is much more than coincidence. My brothers, sisters, friends [if I have any], and others in school don't come close to being so tormented by these dark, menacing shadows who seem to be everywhere I go, trying to make my life miserable and doing a good job of it.*

I was deeply sad about the kid having lost his brother. But I didn't have a thing to do with his death, yet I was being treated rudely because of it. This wasn't just make-believe. Too many students, teachers, parents, and those I went to church with treated me differently. I struggled constantly trying to understand why. Maybe I could change somehow, but I didn't know what needed changing. I never went around looking for trouble. I didn't even go around looking for friends. I just tried to be left alone, and that seemed impossible.

One day in history class, we had a substitute teacher. She was young and quite pretty. She also went to the church I attended. This was good because she knew me and had never been rude to me. I had been to her home on church visits on a few occasions. It was comforting knowing that an adult who wasn't condemning of me was my teacher for a day.

I heard a slapping noise, then felt a sting on the side of my neck. Then there was a flat thud as a wooden ruler landed on the floor next to me. Giggles broke out around the room disrupting the silence. I felt a flush but didn't look around to see who had hit me. I figured that if I didn't know who to be mad at, I could stay a little calm. Though my anger was rising, I just kept studying.

"You pick that up right now and bring it to me," I heard a nasty command.

I looked up, and the teacher was looking at me. I glanced around the room, and the entire class was looking at me with "What are you going to do?" looks on their faces.

I was embarrassed. I wondered why she had spoken to me in that tone.

"Look, I know who you are, and I won't take a bit of crap from you. Do you understand me?" she snarled. "You bring that to me now, or you get out of this class."

Now my anger reached full steam. By my standards, it was never proper to sass an adult. She looked too young though, and she had gone too far.

"I won't bring it to you, but I will leave the class," I scowled. "I don't have to take crap from you either."

I headed up the aisle, and she backed behind her desk. She acted as though she thought I was going to hit her. Her eyes were wide and scared looking. I heard gasps around the room.

"He didn't do anything," someone confessed from the back of the room. "I was flipping a spit wad, and my ruler slipped and hit him. It was an accident, and I'm sorry," he added.

She looked at him, then at me. The class was quiet and frozen. Everyone was waiting for the tension to disperse so that they could breathe.

"You just go sit down," she said nastily.

I went back to my seat. I threw the boy's ruler back to him, and he apologized again.

"You're not going to get even with me after class, are you?"

"No," I promised.

I was upset. My thoughts weren't on him but on the teacher. I looked at her, and she looked away quickly. She didn't look pretty and young anymore. She looked like my fifth grade teacher—the warden: old, ugly, and stern.

My emotions were churning violently. There was no controlling the constant eruptions and torment inside. I was sad, mad, and disappointed all at once. It wasn't right for her to treat me that way. Like everyone, she seemed to be deliberately looking for the chance to humiliate me.

## 24

*He who makes a beast of himself*
*gets rid of the pain of being a man.*

—Dr. Samuel Johnson

I looked forward to track season. I needed something to put some sort of meaning into my life. Running was a perfect way to burn off anxiety. I pushed myself to the limit in each practice to try to get too tired to think or care about anything. All during the track season, my chest would burn with a fiery sensation in my lungs, and I coughed incessantly. The coughing led to severe headaches that would often throb so violently that I couldn't move. With all its discomfort, track helped me to focus away from people around me. Often, if a day had been extremely cruel, I would run harder and longer thinking perhaps I might die. The coach who didn't give me an A in PE in ninth grade had died trying to run too far too fast. Pushing myself in this manner hurt excruciatingly but relieved my sadness and bitterness. Running hard set fire to my feet, calves, chest, and nostrils. Usually, sucking so hard to get enough air became painful and caused muscles to ache in my neck and back. These pains drove me on because they shut the shadows out of my mind. After practice, I would run home about a mile and a half. My shins screamed with pain, and my heart pounded desperately to furnish the lifeblood to my system. Very often tears filled my eyes as I thought of why I must torture myself in such a manner. In meets, I ran where I felt comfortable. I didn't want attention and didn't care much who I beat or who beat me. I just wanted to be closer to first than last.

When districts came, we were told that three places in each event would go to state. I wasn't favored at all to place and didn't care until there was a half lap left in my race. I ran the half mile, which was twice around the track. It was more of a sprint than the 880 run, which it was called. With the half lap left, I looked at the leaders. They were staggering through the last turn with about a quarter of a lap to go. I realized that the kid in third place was dead tired. I decided I'd get a trip to state. My body responded to my desire, and I could feel the power and energy of the work I had done that season. I passed the third man on the last turn into the straightaway. I looked up, and the number 2 man was moving slow. Second would be easy, so I burst harder and stronger. My legs pounded with such ease that I sped up considerably. I passed the guy quickly and looked at the leader. I had a strong feeling that I could catch him even though he wasn't far from the finish. Another burst of energy carried me toward him. I concentrated on the finish line. He was moving so slowly it seemed unreal. Determination gripped my senses and forced me to find another shot of speed. I knew I hadn't run this fast before and enjoyed the feeling of moving so strongly on my own will. I stretched hard and thrust my head and chest forward at the finish line. My concentration was fixed on him as we crossed it. I hit the tape just a fraction before he did. The expression on his face showed that he hadn't been aware of my approach. He had been sure that he had this race won, and I had stolen it from him. I had a strange tickling feeling permeating my whole body. I had accomplished something good. I was amazed at the number of people clapping and cheering for me. I hadn't felt that good in a long time. I was very excited to get home and surprise my parents.

I was put on some relay teams because of my good showing in the 880. In all, I finished the day with four ribbons. This was great. It made me at least partly the athlete I daydreamed at being. After my last race, I put on my letterman's jacket and was in the center of the field looking over my ribbons. I was proud of what I had done. A voice suddenly broke my celebration.

"Oh, how's our big superstar with all those ribbons and fancy jacket?"

The voice was sarcastic and unfamiliar. I looked up to see the redheaded boy who had picked the fight with me my first day of school in Harden, the one who had flipped me with the elastic, who broke my pencil, and who embarrassed me in front of the whole school—the boy who had started all the misery I had experienced during the past few years. He had moved away during the seventh grade, and I hadn't seen him since. I glanced around us, and no one was close by. I stepped in his path and got close to his face.

"You're nothing but a…wimp. If you have any guts, let's go over behind the bleachers." I motioned toward the grandstand. "No one will be there to break up the fight, and I would love to kick the hell out of you," I challenged him.

All the hatred that had now become my companion was surging to pound on him. My entire body was shaking, not from nerves like I usually did but because I wanted so badly to hit him right then and there.

"No, I'm sorry," he apologized. "I really don't want to fight. I know you'd whip me."

His backing off so submissively was surprising to me. He had always been so cocky and mouthy before. He would never have backed down from a fight while he was in Harden. All I did was stare at him as he walked away. I felt ashamed and, for some reason, sad for him.

At home, I jumped the porch railing and rushed into the house. Mom was in the living room, sewing.

"Look what I won," I burst out excitedly. "I'm going to state because I won first in the half mile."

"That's nice," she said dully not glancing up from her task.

I stood looking at her, waiting for her to ask about the meet, the races, and the ribbons. She just kept on sewing.

I thought for a moment that I would tell her how exciting it had been to win the race. Then, I guessed she would probably just tell me to ignore it. I walked away wondering why I was so worthless in her eyes. I could see others treating me that way but not my own mother.

Soon Dad walked through the door. I laid the ribbons out on the table where he couldn't miss seeing them. He walked by without a glance.

*Oh well, he probably didn't see them*, I thought.

"Hey, Dad, look what I won today. I took first in the half mile and am going to state," I said more excitedly hoping for a better reaction than from Mom. Maybe since he was a man, it would mean more to him.

"Hmm," he replied walking away.

I took my ribbons and went to bed. I had thought I had done something good, but they made me feel like a dope. It was hard work, yet it didn't matter to them at all. Even our coaches hadn't reacted too excitedly to my winning, not the way they did when others won or even placed.

My room seemed darker than usual as I pulled the covers over my head and tucked them tightly around me to hide from the world.

At the state meet, I was determined to make a good showing. I was in a great mood the day of my race, and the thrill of watching others win had built my confidence and desire. I would be in a race with a runner whom everyone believed would set a new state record. I decided I'd stay with him and see who could win the sprint at the end.

The race began on a very fast pace. He and I went out from the start and ran side by side. The first lap was under one minute, and I was on course for the fastest half-mile of my life. I had plenty of energy to spare and no fatigue going in the second lap. I could hear people in the stands cheering wildly. Here was one of the best races they'd seen with an absolute unknown tied for the lead. The energy of their noise boosted me. Even though I stayed outside of him, I began to move away. I could see him start to struggle to keep pace. This was supposed to be his race. No one was supposed to be good enough to come close to him. With a half lap left, I looked back at his face. He had a strained worried look. All he had worked for was running away from him. I guessed it was draining his confidence as well as his energy. I listened to the crowd cheering wildly. I thought of his parents and family all there. I had seen them encouraging him before the race. He had a lot of people to make happy. I had none. I imagined the announcement over the intercom at school about me setting a new state record. There would probably be many groans. Our school record was over twenty years old and held by a local businessman. I would shatter his record at this pace, and people wouldn't be happy. I looked back at my opponent again. I slowed a little, and his face lit up. The closer he got, the more energy he seemed to muster. The celebrating belonged to him. I had no right to steal it. I had proven what I could do, and it was easier than I expected. I was the only one who cared that I could do it. I proved to myself that I could win state, and that was enough. I slowed to a jog for the rest of the race. I didn't want second or third place. I didn't care just so I could avoid a crowd. When I crossed the finish line, the winner was surrounded by a happy group of people.

I tried to ignore the fact that I didn't matter to anyone. The thoughts and feelings of loneliness shadowed me everywhere. My fights became daily bouts against despair. I even had guilt feelings because I was an outcast and ignored. *Why should it matter to me?*

I tried to reason. I should have been able to accept me for what I was even if I didn't know what that was. I wondered if I just had a knack for drawing the darkness out of people. Whatever the reasons for my situation, I couldn't comprehend them.

# 25

*Bad tabulation there.*

—Evelyn Waugh

I had loved rainstorms in the past. Now they were depressing and cast a dark gloom over the world. Instead of raindrops being the pure cleansing tears of a tender heaven, they were now darts of condemnation attacking a filthy world. They tore the surface off the mountains, turned patient trickling streams into angry torrents stained with earth's brown blood. They swelled beautiful dark-green rivers into black, threatening serpents hungry to devour everything in their paths. Their constant tap, tap, tapping on the roof and windows tried to lure me outside to let their cold stickiness leave me damp, chilled, and uncomfortable. These storms would come and reign cruelly over my world. They shut me into a lonely, dark dungeon until a bright shaft of light would shine through and unlock the gloom on the mind. But residues of sloppy mud would linger for days sticking to harden and disfigure my soles.

My fight for identity was real, but the entire nature and form of the enemy was more than a mist of confusion. I didn't know where I was or what was needed to free myself.

The remainder of my junior year was overcast. Too many fights, too many threats, and too much hatred. I believe I began to interpret some kids' behavior wrongly. At church one evening, one of my older brother's friends hit me playfully as he had done for years. He was tall, broad, and strong from milking cows by hand. I viewed his aggressiveness toward me as abuse and snarled a severe warning to him. He laughed and slapped my face lightly. I quickly landed a right fist squarely onto his left cheek. His head snapped violently away, and his body hit the wall. Tears welled slowly and rolled down his stunned face. The hand he had sent to nurture his wound caressed a huge red knot as he pulled it away to check for blood.

"I'm telling your brother," he wailed. "He won't let you get away with this."

"Tough crap," I countered. "He doesn't scare me any more than you do. I'd just as soon hit him as you."

I was bitter, mean, justified, and able to make people leave me alone. I wasn't part of their world. Now, they would pay if they trespassed into mine. They had forced me into a closed world, and it was too small and tight. I just couldn't allow myself to be hemmed in any tighter.

Shortly after that incident, the scouts were in front of the church on a Friday afternoon. We were waiting for the scoutmaster to come and take us camping. My brothers had brought along boxing gloves for entertainment.

"Does anyone want to box our brother?" they challenged the group.

I stared around, expressionless. I didn't care. Most of them were bigger than me. No one took the offer. I came on these trips so I could be in the mountains, and that was about all; I didn't care what others did.

"Come on, chickens," the younger of my brothers teased. "Look at him. He's smaller than almost all of you. He's not so tough. We fight him at home all the time," he encouraged.

"I'm not afraid of him. I'll fight him."

I turned to see one of the quietest and most well liked of the group standing to the take the gloves. He always stayed out of the spotlight in everything we did. Why he would accept this was baffling to me. For him, it was very out of character, and I didn't want to fight him. There were plenty of other jerks there that I would rather pound on, guys with big mouths who needed a fat lip.

"Naw," I declined. "I don't want to fight you. You're too nice a kid."

"No way. You guys said anybody, and I'm not a bit afraid of you. You're not so tough as you think you are."

I wondered where this was all coming from. I already regretted that they had brought the gloves. All this could do was reinforce in others their dislike for me. I refused to put the gloves on. The quiet boy protested, then hit me when I declined again.

"Okay," I relented. "At least let me get the gloves on. I don't want to hurt you too bad."

"You won't hurt me. Don't worry," he sneered at me.

I was very surprised. During this short time I had heard him say more than over the previous three years. I didn't want to hurt him. In spite of what he had said, and his tone, I liked him. There had to be some dark and evil influence prodding him into this. As we squared off, I studied him. I ducked a couple punches without throwing one back. He was slow and wild and didn't protect his midsection at all. I hated to do it, but I figured it would be better than marking his face. I faked a left jab at his nose, and when he brought both gloves up to protect his face, I buried a hard right into a soft, unprotected stomach. He gasped a sharp *umph* as air gushed from his body. He started to cough and heave trying to breathe. I watched the teardrops snap loose from his eyes and splash like little bombs onto the sidewalk. His friends grouped around him to offer aid.

"I'm sorry," I said and went around the corner to wait by myself. I had just stacked another brick onto the load of resentment against me in this small town. I was certain it didn't matter what I did though; the resentment would mount without any justifiable cause.

## 26

*All aggressive acts have one thing in common:*
*they justify forceful resistance.*

—Michael Walzer

The last day of school ended with more unwanted attention. I was just stepping on top the first step of the bus when someone grabbed both my shoulders and pulled me away.

"Get out of my way. I'm in a hurry."

I knew the kid. He was two years younger than I. He had a brother a year older, and his father was driving the bus. His Dad was sitting there, watching the incident from the driver's seat, and his brother was in the first seat behind the driver. Even though he was two years younger than me, he was taller and heavier than I was. I moved back in front of him to get onto the bus, and he hit me on the back of the head and then on the shoulder. I saw a look of disbelief on his father's face. I guessed he felt confident with his Dad and brother sitting right there. It didn't matter to me though. When he hit my head, it hurt enough to start the bitter hatred erupting. My stomach boiled and sent steam to my brain. The uncontrollable anger I had become subject to gripped me quickly. Just for an instant, I thought of what might come from behind me, but with little hesitation, I pushed him hard to the side of the bus. I hit him a few times in the face and turned to get onto the bus. His father was there but froze as I turned to him with my fists up and ready. I glanced back at the dork. He was crying, and blood was dripping from above one eye. He had visible white knots on his face.

"I didn't want to fight," I said turning back to his father. "I had nothing to do with starting this."

He shook his head in agreement and went by me to help his kid. He immediately began to berate him for fighting. I got on the bus and headed for the rear as usual. After just a few steps, a girl jumped up and slapped my face. It was hard and hurt a bunch. She was a girl my own age.

"You're such an ignorant jerk," she screamed at me.

I put up my fists and glanced hard at her. She was heavyset, weatherworn like a farm girl, and ugly. Her face was pitted with acne. I could have hit her and felt justified, but I just walked away and sat down. Two unforeseen attacks by such unlikely people and so close together; it all baffled me. Fighting boys was one thing. *What if these girl attacks became regular? How in the world would I deal with that?* I had really wanted to hurt her for an instant, but I knew I would have regretted it later. Not just because of the repercussions from the school kids, but I wasn't sure I could live with myself if I hit a girl.

## 27

*Keep me from giving in to the soft temptation*
*Of sleeping at midday under the open sky,*
*Or taking my ease on a slope nearby a grove.*

—Virgil

The summer began busy as ever. One farmer in particular had hired me full time because he wanted to be sure I would be available when he needed me. Even if he gave me a day off, there was always someone wanting help. I even worked some Saturdays. These had always been reserved for fishing and camping in the past years.

One Sunday at church, we were waiting to begin a young men's class. Our bishop came in and introduced a new teacher to the class. I'd never seen nor heard of him before. He was tall and lean, had a very friendly face, and scholarly demeanor. He looked us over smiling until his eyes met mine.

"Bishop," he said sternly, "isn't this young man the one I have been told of who is a troublemaker?"

"Well, he's that young man, but I've never had any complaints from his teachers at church of any trouble," he defended.

"I'll not teach a class with his kind in it," he said snobbishly.

"What if I guarantee he'll be no trouble?"

"Well, I'll give him one chance," he relented. "But when we meet at my house, he won't be welcome to come there. I don't want his kind on my property."

"I guess that's up to you," the bishop smiled.

"I won't tolerate one bit of trouble from you," the teacher warned pointing a finger at me.

The attention was embarrassing. His finger and face fuzzed in my vision as my eyes became misty. The tension and hatred within me burned to a new height.

"Why, why, why?" my soul screamed. "Everyone in the class knows I am probably the least likely to cause trouble in any of our church classes." I always just sat and listened and tried not to be noticed.

It was common knowledge that the bishop's son was the biggest hellion during church meetings.

After church, the new teacher talked to me about a party at his house on Tuesday evening. He said I could go if I behaved 100 percent. I told him that I was not disrespectful to others on their property but that I wasn't interested in parties and didn't care to go to his. It wouldn't hurt my feelings not being welcome. I wondered what he thought I might do to his house and yard.

That Tuesday, he came to my home to pick me up. He said that he felt it was wrong to let everyone else go and not me. Again, I assured him it was no problem for me, and I didn't really want to go there, especially if it were going to be offensive to his wife.

"No, my wife won't mind at all. She thinks everyone should be treated the same, and she was upset that I hadn't invited you to come. She said all come or none, so I'd like you to come."

"Okay," I said and went with him. I didn't want his conscience bothering him because of me. I also didn't want any couples fighting over how I was to be treated. It would just add to people's disdain for me. I felt uncomfortable going to the stupid party though.

On the way, he asked me questions about the church and acted shocked every time I answered him. At his home, he watched me closely, but I didn't think it was anything more than curiosity. I wondered what people had told him to get him acting so weird. I spent some time outside with him as he showed me his place. It was a nice home with considerable acreage. It was about four miles out of town. He was proud of it, and I told him how I liked it and what I would do on the property if it were mine. He was impressed and surprised. When we went back inside, his wife visited with me for about a half hour. I began to worry that her husband would get upset at my talking to her. She seemed to have a real sincerity in asking about things I liked. I knew she was just being kind though. She was a very pretty lady and fun to talk to. She complimented me on my maturity and values. This was hilarious to me. Everyone knew I was a bad person. I figured once she got to know me better, she would change her mind. Within a few months of their moving there, neither one would probably want to talk to me again unless it was cussing at me for something I did wrong.

After the party, my brothers and I decided to walk home. There were foxes living in the fields between his home and ours, and we enjoyed hiding and watching them play. The teacher again acted stunned. He didn't know he had foxes living close by, and more so he was surprised I could have such interests. When we were leaving, he and his wife told me I would be welcome in their home any time and asked if I would come back often. That puzzled me. I wondered if he was just being nice to make up for having been so rude before.

Near the end of the summer, my brother started trying to coax me to the pit to swim. I was usually too tired or busy. The thought of it also brought back memories, which I didn't care to deal with. That girl was one point that I couldn't protect myself from emotionally. Thinking of her and her onetime kindness made my chest hurt and stormed me with loneliness. I finally went late one afternoon. When I stepped over the edge of the pit to head to the water, I stopped cold and turned to leave. I had caught a glimpse of a girl in a suit and her hair done up cutely. I knew who it was, and I didn't want to be glared at. I headed for the canal to swim home.

"Oh, come on," my brother prodded. "She's not going to bite you. Besides, it's not her pit. We can swim on the other side. I didn't walk all this way just to go back home."

I finally gave in to his persistence. I was churning inside with violent twangs of panic and uncertainty. I liked her too much to be around her and be snubbed. I became very weak as I went down the opposite side of the pit and dove in. Once under the water, I didn't want to come up. I swam to the bottom, and it was icy cold. I tried to stay there fearing her cruel stares or rude remarks. Even if she just got up and walked away, that would hurt worst of all. Suddenly, I realized that I needed air. My lungs and throat started collapsing trying to bring in some oxygen. I looked up and wondered if I'd make it to the top. I was reaching and pulling hard to get there quickly. Some water went through my nose and I choked. I hit the surface coughing and gasping. My mind and vision were still black from the panic. I gasped in a breath before I sank heavily. I pulled and kicked and broke the surface again as I gasped in more fresh air.

"Hey, you need some help?" a sweet voice chimed. She held my arm to give me support, and the warmth of her touch flooded through my cold soul. I started stroking and made my way to the rocky bank. I laughed and blushed terribly when I looked at her. Her hair had been done up so nice, and now it was dangling around her face. I wondered why she had done it up like that just to go swimming.

"Oh, look at my hair," she lamented. "All the time I spent fixing it so I'd look good when you got here."

I looked at my brother. She laughed sweetly.

"I asked him to get you here however he could," she said. "I wanted to see you again."

"Yeah, now kiss and makeup," my brother teased.

I blushed again. The feeling of those hot flushes brought back memories that I had longed for.

I looked back at her. The tight wetsuit outlined a perfect figure. Her eyes sparkled and danced with laughter, and a smile reflected her cheery personality.

*I wouldn't dare touch her*, I thought. She wasn't the girl I had known and been so happy to be around those few years earlier. *She looks so very different now.* As my eyes caressed her figure, I was both excited and ashamed.

"You're not lusting, are you?" she interrupted my awe.

This brought on the worst blush I had ever felt around her. I hadn't been thinking anything that bad. She was just so different, and some strange feelings had brought on a new dimension of attraction to her.

"No," I quickly blurted apologetically. "You just are different than the last time we were here." I clumsily tried to make sure I didn't offend her again.

"Don't worry, I won't slap you for liking what you see," she giggled. "I wanted to look nice so you'd still like me. Do you like my suit?" She posed and turned. "I bought it to impress you."

She certainly knew how to make me blush all the time. I wanted to turn away to hide what felt like a burning face but was frozen on the spot.

"I...I always liked you," I stammered uncomfortably. For having known her so well before, I now felt strangely new at talking to her. It was exciting yet terrifying.

"Boy, what mush," my brother yucked at us. "I'm going to the canal to swim. I'll see you at home," he called back in disgust.

"I really have missed you," she said in a serious tone. "It's been awhile."

She was very different. Her voice was fuller, and her manner wasn't so girlish. I wondered what it was. The word *woman* entered my mind, and I began to feel uneasy. That word and these feelings didn't belong in my world. I wasn't worthy of such things.

"You know what you did was cruel, huh?" she reminded me of the stupid mistake I had made. "But I forgive you, okay? I mean I forgive you if you will forgive me for bearing a grudge for so long."

"I never held it against you," I said. "I wouldn't blame you if you never spoke to me again." I hated the sound of what I had just said, and it sent cold shivers deep into my feelings.

"Oh, but I want to," she insisted, staring into my eyes. She leaned close and whispered, "I like you very much, and I want to get to know you better."

Now I was too nervous to blush. She was close and leaning toward me. I wanted to close my eyes and look away, but I couldn't. Even if I didn't deserve it, I was selfish. She made me feel too comfortably different to reject her kindness and somehow what felt more than kindness. I hadn't enjoyed these feelings for a long time, and I now yearned to keep them. Being close to her was the only way I could. Everything about her penetrated deeply into my emotions—her voice, her forwardness, her kindness, and even her appearance. She looked so wonderfully beautiful standing there in the tight suit with her wet hair dangling in strings along the edges of her face. I had to fight the impulse to reach out and take her hands to draw her closer.

As I stared, I wondered what I should do; she took my hand and drew herself nearer. The cold fingers sent warmth through my cold heart. She stared into my eyes and slowly raised on her toes. I watched her eyes close as she leaned in and touched her lips to mine. The moist warmth reached deeply into my heart and threw open the hardened sealed doors of bitterness.

She opened her eyes. "You should close your eyes when you kiss someone," she gently instructed.

So I did.

## 28

*Under a bad government…equality
is only an appearance and an illusion.*

—Jean-Jacques Rousseau

When football started, I was ready and serious. We had new coaches, and I had grown to five and a half feet and 130 pounds. I wasn't big compared to most, but it felt big to me. I went out for running back and played with a vengeance. I was determined never to let any of those jerks who despised me tackle me. I would pick a hole through the line and then run right at the linebackers. I ran over as many as I could get, then kicked and fought as a crowd of tacklers formed around me. I didn't go down nearly as often as they would. The coaches laughed and jeered at the defense for letting such a little guy hammer them like that. It spurred them on, and the harder they hit, the meaner I got. I wanted to do well enough throughout the season to possibly get a scholarship.

On defense, I played end. I didn't care whom I hit just, so I knocked them down. My teammates would often sneer and yell that we were on the same team. I wondered where they would get that idea. I had never been on their teams even though we played together. I didn't have teammates or friends, except for one. She was all I needed in the world.

I always worked hardest and ran the fastest in practices. After practice when I ran home, I would race to see how quickly I could cover the almost two miles. I was soaring on a new level of strength and desire. Perhaps it all came from one small kiss.

When our first game came, I was on special teams. Surprisingly to me, another boy started at my position at fullback. His father was always at practice and talking with coaches, but I didn't see how that qualified him to start. I was far better than he was. Besides, he was lazy in practice. He ran slow and seldom did all the exercises. We lost a close game, and I never did get in on offense or defense. Our next three games were total blowouts. We didn't score at all, and the opposition all scored in the thirties. I never set foot on the field in those games even though I continued to dominate and improve in practice. After our fourth loss, I handed in my uniform. My Dad didn't even come to the games. There was no way he would be able to practice kissing up to the coaches, so I knew I would never get to play. I hated being used like that, so I quit. I had a job available in the evenings, which paid good money, so it was more profitable to me than sitting on the bench. This injustice swelled me with hatred for the coaches and especially for the lazy kid who got to play just because his Dad was a kiss up. I realized, though, that I had to just ignore it.

Our first game after I quit was a home game. I loved to watch and hope we would get killed. I yearned to play on the teams against us each week. During that first home game, one of my brothers came up crying. He said some big kid had been hitting him. With my emotions already erupting, this just exploded any self-restraint I might have had. I found the bully in the park behind the bleachers. He was about six feet tall, average build, and had long arms. He had bright-red hair and freckles. The instant I challenged his abuse of my brother, he hit me. The blow glanced off the top of my head. I started swinging hard, fast, surging blows. I could see each one land and watched his head jerk back and forth and side to side. The burning hatred flared in me as I saw the ugly face bouncing around off my fists. I drove in harder and faster as he tried to retreat. Suddenly, his arms fell limp to his sides. His face was blank, and his eyes glazed. He staggered around trying to keep his balance. His lips moved, but no sound came out. I hit him hard one more time just to relieve a little more of the anger, which filled my veins. The blow snapped him back to reality.

"You keep your hands off my brothers," I demanded.

"If they bother me, I'll kick their—"

I cut him off abruptly with a hard blow to his mouth.

"Let's just finish it here and now," I added.

"I won't fight anymore," he insisted.

I hit him again on the cheek. His head jerked back, and a knot swelled on the spot. He turned and ran off.

I had a burning hatred for him even as he was running away. I felt no pangs of remorse or sorrow.

Kids at school didn't approve of my relationship with my girlfriend. From the time we had met at the pit, we had grown much closer. I couldn't understand what I did for her, but she put a spark of meaning into my life. She made me be and feel what I had only dreamed of before. I was at least a little normal because I had a friend. We spent as much time together as we possibly could. I loved the hours we would spend just talking. Whether on the phone or together, it lifted me to new heights. I was magnetized by her kindness, her sincere love for me, and even her attractiveness. When we weren't together, just a thought of her would swell my boson with happiness and send electrical pulses to the far reaches of my battled soul. Such peace was more precious to me than anything I had ever known.

She liked to be seen with me at school and liked to hold hands in the halls and hug and cuddle. This was uncomfortable to me because I didn't like people watching me touching her. The shroud of hatred from others, which cloaked my world, outweighed her gentle attention when we were in public. I burned with the fear of attention I felt we drew to ourselves by displaying our affection. It caused me to sweat and tremble. The tension gave me nervous headaches. Kids would greet her kindly, then turn and scowl at me.

"Don't let them bother you," she encouraged me one day. "If people really knew you, they'd like you a lot. It's just hard to get to know you. That scares people. Plus the fact that they are afraid that you would just as soon punch them as say hi."

"Most of them, I would." I smiled, looking into her eyes. Her presence often quelled my feelings of rage and hatred. It was a clean feeling, and I loved it.

"I'm going to have a party at my house one of these days so you can get to know more kids," she assured me.

"I don't like parties," I protested. "Besides, I like being with just you. I don't need any more friends."

"Well, we'll try it anyway," she countered.

Wrestling got off to a terrible start. We had a new coach who had wrestled heavyweight in college and had played on the offensive line for the same school's football team. I didn't know him until our first practice. He was huge and wide from his head to his feet. He had no neck that I could see, and he was very stern. We quickly nicknamed him bulldog because of his looks and build.

We had three grueling days of workouts to begin with, and many kids quit the team. I didn't mind the workouts because I wanted to have my best year. I was excited because this would be the first wrestling coach we had had who actually knew anything about wrestling.

"We're going to vote on team captains today," he announced the fourth day of practice. "I want you to choose two seniors who are clean cut, who represent their school and community well, and who will be good leadership for this team."

After the voting, he tallied the results and told us he would discuss it the next day. When practice was over, he told me to stay. When we were alone, he gave me a shock.

"The team all voted for you. I don't know why, but I don't like it. I don't like guys like you and your brothers, and I don't want you on my team. I'm going to ask you to quit, and you ask your brothers to do the same."

I was scared at first; he was so big, especially up close. Though, I quickly became angry.

"I've lettered three years in a row," I informed him. "I've had one of the best individual records of the team each year. There is no way I'm going to quit. If you do anything to try to force it, I'll get you and this school in trouble. My parents will bring a lawsuit."

I knew that wasn't true. My Mom would tell me to quit and just ignore it. I was desperate. I feared he might call my bluff.

"I won't force you to quit. I just don't like dealing with hoodlums like you," he boomed. "I'll tell you another thing. I don't like wrestlers walking around the school with girls. It gives us a bad image. You're not old enough to be hanging around a girl so much."

He face was a threatening scowl, which caused me to tremble. He looked so mean.

"Another thing," he added. "Don't expect any help from me. I won't do a thing to improve your wrestling. I can't, with a clear conscience, contribute to your fighting in any way, and by teaching you to wrestle, I am contributing to your fighting."

I began to boil again. *Who in the world did this guy think he was? No one could be so perfect as to judge someone they didn't even know the way he was judging me.*

"Well, I'll tell you something," I blurted out. "My girlfriend happens to be the only friend I have in this school. I like her way too much to just brush her off. I don't want to go against your rules or show disrespect to you, but some of your rules aren't your business."

"Just so you know how I feel," he finished.

I went home very upset. The season hadn't even started, and already, I was being robbed and cheated again. I hated that coach, and I was afraid of him. He had no business coming between my girl and me nor did he have any business telling me I couldn't wrestle.

The next afternoon at practice, he announced that there would be three team captains. He then gave his girlfriend spiel to the whole team. At least half the team had steady girls. I was sure he couldn't enforce that rule. I couldn't imagine anyone in their right mind dumping a girl for some big ugly wrestling coach, and no one did.

With the captain situation, he let me be one, but during that year, he didn't let me ever go out at the beginning of matches as the team captain. The other two, who were seniors, always went.

At 130 pounds, I could beat anyone on our team, including the heavyweight. Until he realized this, the coach tried to use bigger wrestlers to abuse me. He would get furious and yell at the large ones when I would pin them. One of my brothers was the second best wrestler on the team. If he had had any self-confidence, he would have been the best. He had great talent and strength but very little self-esteem. When the coach started picking on him, he went downhill. He wrestled in a weight class in which there was a boy whom the coach adored. They were almost immediately like father and son. The kid wasn't that good of a wrestler, so the coach wanted my brother out of the way so his pet could wrestle varsity. During practices, the coach would be very abusive of my two brothers and me. He always made us wrestle with him, and he would lay on us in a manner that prevented us from breathing. The brother he wanted out of the way finally quit the team.

In spite of his abuse and efforts to ruin my season, I lost only one match. That one I lost by a point. At the district meet, I was seeded first and had a bye the first round. I pinned my next two opponents with our coach on the sideline rooting for them to beat me. In the championship match, I knew my opponent would come out hard at first. I always had a slow start but finished strong. His coach would try to get him to take advantage of that to finish the match quickly. I was prepared for a quick attack by him. It bothered me though when I saw my coach talking with his coach and the ref just prior to our match.

When the ref blew his whistle, my opponent charged and just tried to tackle me. I wanted to jump back, spread my legs, and drive my forearm to the back of his neck pushing him to the mat. The heel of my shoe caught in the mat though, and I fell backward. He crawled up my body to gain control, and I bridged and rolled sideways as I hit the mat. The instant my shoulders touched, the ref blew the whistle and called me pinned. An opponent is supposed to have control of you and hold you down for three seconds for a pin. I jumped up complaining to the ref. I looked to my coach for help, and he was laughing. I looked back to the ref, and he was smiling at my coach. I was sure they must have set it up, so I decided the only thing I could do was ignore it. I was still filled with the pangs of being cheated again. This time though, it hurt much more. I had wanted that title desperately and had worked hard so I could have it.

At the state meet, I played around in my first match and tried moves that I had seen but never used. I couldn't find the heart or desire to work at it. I wanted to win, but I felt dull and out of sync. The kid I wrestled was easier than most I had wrestled that season, but I just couldn't find the desire to win. A number of times I could have pinned him but just let him go. He won by a point, and my wrestling was over. I left the mat empty and saddened. If anyone had cared at all, I was sure I could have done well at state. Not even my girlfriend cared though. She didn't like anything to do with fighting and believed that wrestling contributed to my fighting all the time. She had watched one match during the year because it was on my birthday.

I had hoped that I would at least get a small college offer to wrestle, but I heard from no one. I knew nothing of this process for getting scholarships. I figured that someone would just come offer me one. During that summer, I was told that our coach had bragged around that some schools had contacted him about me and he had vigorously discouraged their interest. It really disgusted me to think that someone who thought they were so righteous would think it was okay to play God with another person's life that way.

At the athletic awards banquet, the coach got up to present the most outstanding wrestler of the year award. Though I was the only team member with over six wins during the regular season and I had placed highest in district, I knew he wouldn't give me any recognition. We were all on the auditorium stage in front of the student body while he praised whom he was about to give the award to. Most of the guys were looking or pointing at me, which embarrassed me tremendously. I was sure the award would go to one of the other team captains. Instead, he gave it to his pet, who had had a losing record that season. In fact, he shouldn't have even been on varsity. The coach had made my brother quit, so his pet could be on varsity. Of all the low and sick thinks that had happened to me in wrestling, this one drove me to a new level of disgust and anger. I swelled with bitterness and wanted to run forward and knock the smile off his little pet's face as he took the trophy. And the coach, in my mind, was no more than a coward like the one I had my sophomore year. What a stinking hypocrite. If he had any guts at all, he would have told the student body he was giving the award to the worst varsity wrestler and the one who kissed up to him the most. The whole thing was disgusting and perverted. I didn't feel embarrassment at not getting any recognition though. I was the only four-year letterman in my graduating class and had earned more varsity letters than anyone else. None of this was mentioned. I knew if one of the popular boys had done what I had in athletics, he would have been recognized for his accomplishments. I wished I could ignore it, but it hurt deeply.

With the end of wrestling, the darkest of shadows flowed in to cement my miseries in Harden. What exactly happened, I can't pinpoint. Nevertheless, things changed drastically.

Just before the end of wrestling, I had gotten into a fight with another wrestler. He died in a freak accident two weeks later. This increased some of the mutual hatred toward me. I heard almost every day that one big dork or another was going to beat me up. None of them ever approached me though.

At a youth dance at church, I got in a fight with another farm boy. He was stocky and very solid. He had pushed me so I had hit him in the mouth. We went outside to fight and while I was taking off my coat, he hit me twice. My right cheek burned with pain, and I could taste blood in my mouth. I had a hard time dodging more punches before I got my hands free from the sleeves. His cheap shots and the pain had stoked the rage within me. I felt bitter most of the time now, and it took very little to set me into a rage of violence. I started swinging furiously and with more desire to do serious hurt than I had ever felt before. Blow after blow landed solidly on his face. He was trying to cover up and back away, and my upper cuts would stand him up for more punishment. Someone grabbed me around the waist from behind and spun me away from my victim.

"We'll have none of this here," a voice said.

I looked into the dark eyes of a young guy in his early twenties. He was heftily built but not much taller than I was.

"If I catch you at this again, I'll beat you both up," he threatened.

I knew him from church and was sure I could whip him easier than I could the other boy; I thought about it momentarily, then brushed it aside. He was a nice fellow who lived down the road from us and came from a good family.

While I was looking at him pondering what to do, the other boy ran up and hit me again. The man who broke up the fight shoved him hard into the building and threatened to beat him to a pulp. I wondered how it made any difference whether I did it or he did. We went our separate ways, and I just decided to drop it. Being hit now didn't feel the way it used to. It just seemed like a normal part of life, like cutting myself shaving or just bumping into people in a crowded hall.

The next night, I got in a fight during a church basketball practice. A boy had gotten upset because I kept stealing the ball from him. The next time he got the ball, he threw it in my face. It tore my skin away from my mouth and nose sending sharp pain through my head. My eyes blurred, and my mind seared hot with a desire to hurt him. I immediately charged him, hitting him twice in the face and knocking him to the floor. I stood over him without a word waiting for him to rise so I could hit him again. Our supervisor rushed over and pulled me away. He scolded me for the incident but said nothing to the other boy. When someone mentioned that the other boy had started it, the supervisor fed me some line of bull about not having to always react to insults and injuries.

"Haven't you heard of turning the other cheek?" he asked.

"Sure," I retorted. "Does that mean if I give him a free hit, then I can beat the crud out of him?" I was serious, but the supervisor acted like I was just being mean. I had to stand and listen to him chew me out, then just went back to playing. I wondered how adults could be so stupid and unreasonable. My actions and reactions seemed so sensible that it was odd that they couldn't see why I did what I did.

On Sunday, I was taken to the bishop's office and lectured again.

"We can't have you fighting all the time," he said. "You cause too much trouble at church. I've been thinking about asking you not to come anymore. Also, if you get into one more fight, you won't be allowed to play basketball anymore."

"Okay," I replied. "I'll try to keep out of trouble." I really intended to try.

The next Thursday, we had a game at a church out in a farming area. During the game, a boy on the other team had pushed me and taken some cheap shots with his elbows. I tripped him once as he headed up the floor, and the refs didn't see it. When he came to warn me about it, I swore at him viciously. After the game, my brother who was only thirteen at the time and I were waiting outside for everyone else to finish dressing. The other team was all outside in a huddle, and I could hear them encouraging the boy I had tripped to come over and hit me. They said they would all protect him if I did anything. I was very nervous not because this boy was over six feet tall and outweighed me by thirty or forty pounds, but because their whole team was coming. I sent my brother in to hurry the others. Even with them, we were outnumbered about thirteen to six. When their team reached me, they formed a circle around me and their chosen fighter.

"Come on, hit him," someone encouraged the kid. "Look how little he is. How can you be afraid of someone that small?" The boy started getting his courage up, and I worried more.

"You take back what you said in there," he demanded.

"Oh, screw you," I told him.

"I'm going to hit you if you don't take it back," he warned.

I saw my brother with the other boys. This made me feel a bit better. I figured if I didn't scare most of their team, we'd all get beat up.

"Oh, just shove it you—" I cursed him again.

He put up his fist to hit me, and I swung a hard right. My adrenalin must have been super high because when I hit him, it lifted him off the ground, onto the hood of the car we were by, and blood splattered the windshield. He rolled off, hit the ground, and stood up woozily at the prodding of his friends. I picked him up and lifted him over my head. His body was in a horizontal position above me. How I was able to lift him is past my understanding. I slammed him onto the pavement with all the force I could summon. He screamed in pain and made a sickening gurgling noise. While he was rolling around moaning, his friends were all standing with their mouths ajar.

"Move," I ordered as I began to drag the kid to the lawn. They all obeyed quickly, and I dragged him over the snow and left him. The pure white snow was shadowed with a dark stain in the pale light.

*Well, that's the end of basketball for me,* I thought as we drove away.

Again, on Sunday, I was called to the bishop's office.

"I realize that sometimes protecting yourself is necessary," he lectured. "I was told what happened, and I won't count that one against you. I would probably have done the same thing. However, I warn you that I won't tolerate anymore."

"Thanks," I said as I left. I was very surprised. *Why would he give me a second chance? He had made it plain that he didn't like me being around the other kids at church. He said that I was a bad influence.*

## 29

*"Wretched Catullus, you should stop fooling*
*And what you know you've lost admit losing.*
*The sun shone brilliantly for you, time was,*
*When you kept following where a girl led you."*

—Catullus

Things were going sour between my girlfriend and me. She was a happy, friendly person and always talked and visited with just about everyone. It hadn't bothered me before, but now I felt a surge of jealousy every time I saw her talking to another guy. I was never happy. I hated her touching me at school. She liked to put her arm around my back as we walked the halls. It annoyed me to the point of panic. Every time she did it, I would sweat and blush and have awful thoughts and feelings of evil eyes looking at me. I began to hate it. I couldn't stand even holding her hand in public. She was hurt more than insulted by my behavior, yet she still went with me to places away from people. We would talk and argue about my behavior. I disliked discussing it, so I just quit seeing her. It hurt me profusely. Each time I saw her at school, I yearned to talk to her and hear her kind voice. Not being able to be with her yet seeing her so often caused me great anguish. All the old stone walls began building up around me. Cold, cruel shadows followed me everywhere I went. I didn't cower from them though. I lashed out at everyone and everything.

I had always enjoyed walking alone outside during snowstorms. It was so peaceful, and the beautiful white of it all gave me a sense of cleanness. I could think, relax, and enjoy myself without others around. Often I would walk for hours and go home refreshed and happy.

But now, since we had broken up, the snow was depressing. I walked out one evening when large white flakes were gently fluttering to the ground. These walks had so often refreshed me and reminded me of her kindness. She seemed so pure and white, like these soft snowflakes. Now some landed on my bare face leaving a frosty bite before melting. The longer I walked, the lonelier I became. Soon tears forced themselves through my hardness and left icy paths down my cheeks. My throat tightened, and my chest ached. I sobbed a little, then more, and finally broke out crying uncontrollably. *Why was I so alone?* The loss of her friendship and closeness now tore through me more than at any time. I couldn't justify my staying away from her, nor could I justify clinging to her gentleness. We didn't fit together, and I didn't want to cause her to suffer. I had never felt so dark and bitter. A deep yearning for her companionship made me hope she would drive by and rescue me from such a forlorn world. *Why couldn't I have any friend, anyone at all to share my feelings with?* I cried so hard I became too weak to walk. I dropped into a snowdrift and screamed for help. No one answered. No one heard. No one cared.

I cried until I was sore from it. My face stung from frozen tears and cold air. My stomach muscles ached from the constant tightening, and my hands and feet throbbed from the unmerciful coldness of the night. I tried to reason that I should be able to control my loneliness. I didn't need friends. Perhaps if I had never felt the kindness and love from one caring person, I wouldn't desire that friendship now. But if everyone would just leave me alone, I wouldn't have to be such an outcast. If they could be content to just not like me and let it go at that. Instead, they had to remind me constantly with glares or comments. I couldn't live through this morbid smothering solitude. I hurt so badly that I prayed it would end. I wished I could fall asleep and just be found, a cold hard corpse the next morning. I still had a faint belief that God was against it though. I cried to him for some strength and help. It made me feel guilty. If I was so bad in the eyes of those around me, I must be even more awful in God's eyes.

The coldness of the snowdrift and the prodding of a sudden wind froze my confused emotions. I knew there had to be an answer somewhere.

Walking home, I decided on a plan. I would study hard and bring up my grades. With a good showing the final quarter, I might be able to get into college. Then I could participate in sports as a walk-on. I got home cold, tired and determined. I was physically and emotionally exhausted, but I had to rise above it all. I would begin to pursue a new course and stay away from people.

## 30

*Again I considered all travail, and every right work,*
*that for this a man is envied of his neighbor.*

—Ecclesiastes 4:4

My decision to start taking school seriously seemed to annoy my parents. After school, I began to hit the books hard each night. When Mom would see me, she would tell me to go do one chore or another.

"Why don't you let me study?" I complained to her one day.

"Can't you find something better to do?" she asked. "Why waste your time with that."

Dad was worse. He would come home and see my studying and start harassing me. He often grabbed my scalp with his fingers, squeezed hard, and jerked his hand away. He did this in quick succession till I would finally complain that it hurt and to knock it off. Then he would slap, kick, or hit me for being disrespectful to him. I began to hate him more intensely. When I would go to my room to study, the two of them would constantly send one of the other kids down to bring me upstairs. After a month of this, I quit trying. Their treatment, however, had hardened my bitterness and magnified my hatred to all around me. Everyone was my enemy. Even the girl who had meant so much to me became an eyesore to me. Instead of memories of kindness, I sensed that I had been used and was now being made fun of. Each time I saw her, darts of pain would cripple my heart and mind.

My high school days were nearing their end, and it all came with a flurry of twisted events. Whatever or whomever had made me a target, opened the gates to flood ultimate misery into my last days of school. Conversely, though, at the very end, there were a couple of bright patches of sunshine.

One afternoon in PE, we were playing flag football. I ran the ball, and a huge kid grabbed my shorts and tackled me, pulling my shorts down in the process. I threatened him as I turned to huddle up.

"You don't scare me, jackass," he hollered.

I turned, ran at him, and shoved him hard. He didn't move an inch, but I bounced back and fell to the ground.

"Oh, tough boy," he taunted.

I glared at his six two, two-hundred-thirty-pound frame. I knew he wasn't afraid to fight because I had seen him fight before. I wondered what my chances would be.

"You gonna chicken out?" he laughed.

That elevated my anger beyond control. I ran at him and hammered him in the mouth with all the hatred I had stored within me. I glared at him, craving another shot. He lifted a hand to the swelling mouth and pulled it away to see a little blood.

"Okay, I don't want to fight." He sniffed.

The following week when we went to the locker room to shower, I got into another fight. The coach had put papers down on the benches with information for a PE test. I picked one up, and it was faded, and the writing smeared. I put it down and picked up the one next to it.

"That's mine," a boy yelled from behind me.

I didn't realize he was addressing me. Suddenly, I was lifted from the floor and was slammed repeatedly against a locker.

"You took my paper," the attacker was screaming.

A few boys grabbed him and pulled him away from me.

"What's the fuss in here?" the coach demanded.

"He took my paper," the boy yelled.

"There's no name on these papers," the coach said. "Everyone just grab one. They all say the same thing."

I looked at the kid. He was about eight inches taller than I was and had a somewhat muscular build. He was the boy from church whose mother had been the principal at the elementary when I had gotten in trouble for not having lunch. There were papers all around the locker room, so how in the world he figured the one I had was his puzzled me. These weird things overwhelmed me. I couldn't understand what it was about me that attracted so much trouble. This boy wouldn't have reacted that way to anyone else.

My forehead was scratched and stinging, and my ribs were the same. He had long fingernails, and they had dug deep.

"I'm going to kick your butt for this," I promised him.

"Oh, wow, I'm really scared," he sneered. "We'll finish it at the youth meeting tonight at church."

"You got it," I said. "Don't you dare chicken out because I'm going to finish this."

"Don't worry. I doubt you can hurt me," he said confidently.

I wondered if he might have a point. He had picked me up so easily and tossed me around like a doll. I was amazed at his strength.

At church, we met outside where only a few kids were around. He came snarling at me as soon as we looked at each other. He was making a low growling sound like a mad dog. I met his approach with a wild flurry of punches. I wasn't about to let him get a hold of me. I would swing hard a few times, then step back and to one side to get a fresh start and avoid his grabbing me. He moved clumsily and slow. It was obvious that he wasn't used to fighting. Once in a while, I could feel a stinging pain on my arms and neck where his fingernails would get a grip and rip away the skin. We fought for quite some time. It must have been at least twenty minutes. I had hit him abundantly, and he was heaving and gasping for breath. My arms were heavy and tired. I dropped them to shake off the weakness, and he lunged in and wrapped his arms around me, locking my arms to my side. I fought hard to free myself and couldn't break his hold. I decided to try to throw my weight and roll. If he were falling, he would probably let go. My wrestling skills helped here. I wanted to be sure he landed on the bottom so I could put a lot of thrust into him as he hit. I didn't care how bad it hurt him. I tried to bend and squat to break his grip, but it didn't budge. Finally, I stomped hard on one of his feet, then kicked hard off the ground. I dropped all of my weight backward and twisted as we were going down. He thudded on his back with me on top of him and groaned terribly. But he didn't release his grip. He easily rolled me over and held on tight. I fought and twisted till his grip finally broke. I then quickly rolled away from him. When he got up, I started swinging again. He began to cry in an awful tone, so I backed off and asked if he wanted to quit.

"Yes," he sobbed. "I don't know why I did this. I'm sorry."

"Come into the bathroom, and I'll help you wash up and put cold towels on your face. It will help you feel better," I offered.

"Okay," he stammered through his tears. When I started cleaning his face, I got sick. It was covered with lumps and small cuts. It looked like he had bounced off the pavement a hundred times. I welled with sorrow for him and told him how badly I felt. He didn't respond. There were a few kids like him around. They were so pampered that they didn't realize that others had feelings too. Whenever they needed attention, it was there immediately.

When I looked into the mirror, my own pain came to life. So far, I had ignored it; now my face burned from deep scratches where chunks of skin had been torn away by his fingernails. As I bathed them with water, fire burned across my face.

I went from the bathroom straight outside. I didn't want any of the leaders to see me. I would be blamed for this whole thing, so I wanted to let it happen at home where my Dad would at least listen to my side of the story. I doubted the boy I had whipped would say anything in my defense. He would bask in the attention this brought to him.

Outside, I met the dark-haired boy who had caused so much misery in the sixth grade.

"Man, you are fast and tough," he marveled wide-eyed. "I sure wouldn't want you mad at me now," he added. "You were pounding him for thirty minutes and didn't even get tired. I've never seen anything like it."

"Don't worry," I said. "I don't fight little kids like you."

He laughed, and I went home. I got into bed quickly in case someone came. I knew Mom would tell them I was asleep. I didn't wait long however. I heard a knock upstairs, and someone said my name.

My Dad was in the next room working. I heard him say, "In there," and in came one of the bishop's counselors. He spoke in a real low tone as he leaned over the end of my bed.

"How dare you pick on such a nice and innocent boy?" he hissed through his teeth. "I ought to drag you out of that bed and beat the hell out of you."

I didn't say a word. I just watched him leave. I wanted to jump up and kick the hell out of him. I was sure I could, but I was afraid my Dad would kill me. I could see people abusing me at church, but they had no right to come into my home, especially into my own bedroom, to threaten me that way.

"What did he want?" my Dad asked through the door.

"He said he wanted to drag me out of bed and beat the hell out of me," I replied calmly.

"Why that son of a—" my Dad shouted. "Who does he think he is?"

Dad ran up the stairs. I knew that look and that he'd beat the guy up if he caught him. I hoped he would. I wanted a little vengeance for all the unfair treatment I had always gotten.

Soon he came back down and asked me what had happened. I explained the whole thing to him as honest as I could.

"Why didn't you tell me he was in here threatening you?" he snapped angrily. "No one has a right to come into my home and threaten my kids."

"I didn't think it would matter that much," I said softly, expecting to get slapped for saying it.

Dad went upstairs, and I could hear him on the phone. He wasn't nice, and he made some sincere promises if that guy ever touched me. I was glad he cussed the guy out, but I was sure he was more angry because the guy had invaded his home…not his son.

At school the next day, the old, grubby farm boy came up to me again.

"I heard about your fight last night," he bragged. "I still want to fight you."

"Well, let's go at it," I said with a smile. "The longer you wait, the worse I'm going to pound you when we do fight."

He laughed and strolled off.

For the first time, I felt a friendship toward him. I didn't know why, but I liked that weird kid.

I didn't go to church the next Sunday. This was one of the few times Dad let me miss. He seldom went but always made us kids go.

The next Tuesday at youth meeting, I was back in the bishop's office. He lectured me about doing serious injury to someone by beating up on them. He tried to tell me some story about a fight he was in when he was my age. I didn't care and didn't want to hear it. They never asked my side of what had happened. I was always guilty. Anyone could pick a fight with me, and that was just fine. They had good reason because I was a bad boy. I didn't count. But it was always my fault.

While I was in listening to him, a friend of my brother's had picked a fight with the scoutmaster's son. He had hit him once and broken his collarbone. I didn't know about it until the next Sunday. I did know about something else though. This same boy and my brothers were harassing my old girlfriend and her new buddy. My brothers knew how I still felt about her even though I never talked about her. They figured they were doing me a big favor by bugging them. They had gotten orange pop and baking soda and dumped it all over the seats of his car. He didn't dare do anything because he was afraid of me. When I went outside, she came and grabbed my hand gently and stared into my eyes. She had tears in her eyes, and she spoke kindly and tenderly.

"You know how I feel about you," she spoke with much emotion. "I still feel that way. You mean more to me than any of the boys I know. You've just changed too much. I'd still go out with you if you wanted, but I don't think you want to. I don't mean that you don't care about me. I know you do. There's just something in you that won't let us be together. It hurts me more than you can know. I cry often because we can't be together like we were before."

I choked as her words knifed into my heart. It would have been easier if she had just said she hated me. I ached to be normal. I would even ask her to marry me. I wanted to ask her right then. The thought of losing her forever doused what little light was left in my soul. I knew I was too different and had too little control over my emotions. I could be nothing but misery to her. My heart screamed, and my soul mourned. This would be our final good-bye. Anguish consumed my entire body. Letting her go was like ripping out part of me. I wanted to throw my arms around her and say I would be anything she wanted me to be. The bitter, cold part of me, the part that controlled me, wouldn't allow me to do anything.

I knew her friend well. In the ninth grade, he had been the basketball star of our school. Now, because of politics, he didn't even make the team. I had nothing against him, but it tore me to see them together. He had even asked me if I minded him dating her before they ever went out.

"Would you please make them leave us alone?" she interrupted my pain.

"Yes, I will," I said sadly. "I didn't put them up to this, and I guarantee they won't bother you again."

After I spoke to them, they apologized.

My brothers liked her too and thought they were doing the two of us a favor.

She came and said that she loved me, and I went home. I was sad that night but couldn't cry. It wouldn't be right. I wondered if it could really be possible for anyone to love me.

At church on Sunday, I was called to the bishop's office. He was very incensed about the boy's collarbone.

"I was in here talking to you when it happened," I protested. "That happened while I was in here Tuesday."

I was frustrated. It was bad enough to be blamed for every fight I got in whether I started it or not, but to be blamed for something I had nothing to do with was absurd.

"I know," he said with an air. "Indirectly, though, you are responsible for everything bad that happens here."

*Boy, what a cowardly way to deal with a problem.* I couldn't even answer his stupidity. I left his office and didn't speak with him anymore. It really ripped me to know he had the nerve to treat me that way when everyone knew his son was the biggest dope pusher in town.

# 31

*How oft, by Allah's will, hath a small force vanquished a big one.*
*Allah is with those who steadfastly persevere.*

—The Quran

Like most schools, we had a section where the rowdy kids sat during basketball games. No girls sat there. It wouldn't be fitting. My friend and I sat on the top row of the bleachers in the bad section. I probably hollered and cussed more than anyone else. I don't know why I was so obnoxious. I felt winning was important though, and I got into yelling for our team and against the other team and the refs. I never thought of the attention I might draw to myself. I'd sat there in the same place for three years and yelled and cussed all the time.

During the game, a ref had made an obvious error when a ball hit an opposing player and went out of bounds. He gave the ball to the opposition, and I erupted in a string of very bad language. I imagine others did too, but I was loud and furious. During this tirade, I got the strange feeling of being watched. I looked over a ways and three rows down. A girl, who just happened to be one of the nicest and kindest in our school, was looking at me. She was very pretty with long, sandy hair and the eyes, face, and smile of an angel. She always wore long but stylish dresses to school. When I would see her, I always felt like I should be ashamed to be allowed where she was, but her nature was such that I could feel no judgment from her. Looking at her, inspired peaceful feelings within me. At this game, she was sitting with a boy who had been our varsity quarterback. Why she would be with such a jerk was a mystery. He was a cocky, no-talent kid who had the right parents and good looks, nothing more. This girl was way too good for him. Besides, I couldn't believe he would bring her to the skuzzy section to sit. That showed his lack of respect toward this girl.

As our eyes met, she smiled a kind, sweet smile. They sparkled, and her face glowed. I was sure she had to be from heaven. Knowing she had heard me swearing was very distressing for me. I felt I had defiled something pure. I wanted to look away, but the strength of her gaze held my eyes to hers. I sat down and couldn't speak; I had no desire to yell or swear or even feel rowdy. A soothing relaxed mood swept cleansingly through my body and mind. I wanted to be ashamed but couldn't. I sat still and quiet the rest of the game.

She looked at me one more time and smiled so kindly again. I was sure she was speaking through her eyes acknowledging her approval of my new feelings. *How wonderful it would be to have a friend like that*, I thought. *What could shadows do around her?*

After that incident, I very seldom swore. I got anxious and excited at games but kept it mostly to myself. Her look and those feelings clung desperately to my harsh personality. However, they weren't enough to curb my rages.

A short time later, I got into a fight with a boy who had been picking on one of my younger brothers. He was a city kid. He was heavier and slightly taller than I and very slow. We fought for about five minutes when I hit him with a cracking right to the left temple. His arms dropped, and he began to stagger and sway. He had two friends with him who hauled him away. Somehow, after this fight, I felt satisfaction instead of guilt; I also felt pride instead of fear. I wasn't shaking as I usually did. I was pumped up and ready for another fight.

The following week, another boy over six feet and quite heavy had walked up behind one of my brothers and kneed him in the back. I was close by and saw my brother fall to the ground gasping for breath and turning purple with pain. The rage within me sent me on a dead run. I jumped and landed both palms on the bigger boy's chest. Just as quickly as I had attacked, I was on the ground. I had just bounced off him. He laughed and came at me. I got up quickly and began to swing wild and furious. I could feel the hard crunching blows land on his face, and after a solid blow to his nose, I stepped back to survey the damage. As soon as I backed away, he kicked a wild shot at my groin. His long, powerful leg landed a huge foot inside my right thigh as I turned to avoid the direct hit. There was no pain, but when I tried to put weight on that leg to stand, it buclked crumbling me to the ground. I quickly pushed away with my left leg. Just when my body jerked backward, I felt a sting on my forehead as another kick barely made contact. I jumped up and in at him swinging as fast as I could move. My leg held up, and I was again making solid contact with my punches. He backed away, and I followed with a series of hard rights to the left side of his face. He staggered and dropped his arms to his side. His eyes rolled and became glazed, and a friend close by grabbed hold to keep him from falling.

"Timber," hollered my brother form behind me. "Serves you right, you jerk."

I was still moving in but was pushed back by his friend.

"He's had enough. Please don't hit him again," he protested. "You made your point."

"All I did was stop a bully form picking on someone half his size," I countered. "I didn't start this. He did."

"I won't argue that, but you could hurt him seriously if you hit him anymore."

I wanted one more punch just to be sure he got the message but wasn't sure he would feel it anyway. Besides, his friend was broader and stronger than he was, and I didn't know if I wanted to fight with him or not.

On Saturday evening, my friend and I were out driving around town late at night. One of the big cowboys drove by, and my friend offered me a challenge.

"If you can whip him, I'll buy you a pop and a candy bar," he said laughing.

I laughed too.

"No, really," he added seriously. "He was talking about you in our Ag class and said there was no way a little snot like you could whip him."

"Okay," I accepted. "You get him to fight, and I'll do it."

He stopped the cowboy and asked him why he had been bad-mouthing me.

"I never said a thing about you," he sneered at me. "I'll tell you though. I'm sure not afraid of you."

"How about if we go for it then?" I challenged.

"That's fine with me. Let's go," he shot back.

We drove to a parking lot behind the elementary school. I walked close and looked up at him. My throat knotted. This guy was extra, extra large. His fists were wide, and his feet were bigger than his mouth. If he hit me with those hands, I would probably go sprawling. Even though I had a twinge of guilt for fighting on a bet, I reached up and punched him hard. I wanted to be sure I hit him at least once. He threw an awkward right, which lowered his head, and I teed off on the target. One after another, I felt hard, unchallenged punches halt solidly against his large face. These punches jolted my arms more than in other fights. His head didn't snap around so much. He was almost like hitting a brick wall. I worried that I might break my hand. I hoped he would give up quickly. I wasn't fighting him on hatred or vengeance, and my arms were tiring. He reached out to grab me, and I dodged and landed a hard shot to his nose. I could see water filling his eyes, but I knew he wasn't crying. He lunged again and got hold of me. I pulled one of his elbows down and threw him over my hip in one of my favorite wrestling moves. Once on top of him, I put a fist in his face.

"I know I can beat you in wrestling," I taunted. "If you want to wrestle, I'll take you down and pound your face in."

"Okay, we'll just box," he panted.

He was really sucking air, and his face had red welts peppered all over it. His right eye was swollen and bruised.

We got up, and he threw another awkward punch. It dropped his left side low and open. I hit him with three solid rights to the left cheek and then started swinging hard and fast again. After a very long flurry of punches, I backed away. His face looked horrible. There were bruises all over it. A small trickle of blood was creeping from his nose, and I could see strings of skin and blood on his lips.

*How stupid*, I thought. *I can't believe I'm doing this. Why would I be so cruel to anyone?* I had been proud that I hadn't gone looking for fights. I thought I always had a good reason. But this was wrong, and I hated it. I didn't like myself for doing it, especially over a stupid bet.

His left eye was puffed shut and bruised badly. Tears were pouring from his eyes, probably from pain, and he hadn't even hit me once. It all began to sicken my stomach.

"Why don't we quit this?" I offered. "I'm getting tired of pounding on your face."

"I'm not quitting," he insisted. "I'm not going to let you go around bragging that you beat me."

"That's fine," I answered him. "You tell people you won if you want, but I'm not going to keep demolishing your face. You can't even protect yourself. You're so tired you can't hold your hands up, and your face is a pulverized mess. You can't hardly breathe. Now don't be so stupid, and let's quit."

"Fine, we'll call it a tie then," he compromised.

"That's fine with me."

I got my pop and candy bar. My friend and I joked about it, but inside, I was mortified. There was nothing uplifting in what I had done.

The next day, I saw the cowboy; his left eye and cheek were horribly black. I hoped it hadn't done any eye damage. I had never seen a black eye like that. His girlfriend was an acquaintance of mine and approached me about the fight.

"You did that to him, didn't you?" she demanded.

"Did he tell you that?" I asked.

"No, he said he hit a door. That's bull, and everyone knows it. You're the only door around here that hits like that. Someone at school said they saw you two fighting."

"He probably hit a door," I said walking away.

Any time anyone showed up at school with a black eye, fat lip, or whatever, I was blamed for it. I was more unpopular at school than I had ever been. I got stares and glares of hate constantly. If I stared back, they would mostly turn away in fear. I heard many whispers each time I walked down the shadowy halls of our school. I began to wonder how safe it was for me to go anymore.

Shortly after the fight with the cowboy, there was a dance in the gym for the last two hours of school. I was sitting in the bleachers watching when a few cowboys came over. One a little bigger than I has told me there was no way I could be as tough as people said.

"I know you couldn't have done to our friend what you did unless you had help," he snorted. "I want you to come outside with me right now."

"With you or all of you?" I asked sneering back.

"I'm going to fight you myself," he assured me.

"Na, I'm trying to quit. Besides, I don't fight at school."

"Well, let's go across the street," he suggested.

"Sorry," I answered back. "I'm not going to fight."

He walked away. This surprised me. He seemed like he really wanted to fight, but he gave up too easily.

When the bell rang, I was in a crowd as we filed out through the gym door. I felt a sharp, stabbing pain in my left leg. I jumped and almost knocked over the girl in front of me. I caught her fearful eyes and apologized as she stared at me.

When I turned, the cowboy who had wanted to fight was holding a pin and laughing.

"I knew you were chicken," he taunted.

I swung around and hit him hard in the chest. Then I shoved him to the floor. He jumped up, and I drove both palms into his chest once more. Kids had opened around us, and the last blow had lifted him from his feet and landed him hard on his can. He bawled in pain as I headed for him.

"Okay, let's head outside and finish this," I snarled.

"No thanks. I've changed my mind," he sissied out.

The next day, I was told he had a broken tailbone. The cowboys were a proud group, and I worried that retaliation would come.

## 32

*Your feelings are understandable. But you*
*should work*
*for a condition where you will not be*
*preoccupied with yourself*
*and your own feelings of inadequacy and can give your*
*entire concern to others.*

—Boyd K. Packer

Our basketball team made the state tournament, and we were going to have our second game on Saturday evening. My friend and I were driving to the state university to watch it. He had too much to drink on the way there and was being very obnoxious and obvious, so I took him to the highest and most secluded spot in the gym. The game wasn't going well, and that had gotten him bouncing around till he got sick and vomited. Some of it had gotten on my letterman's jacket. That jacket meant a lot to me, and this upset me. He had passed out so I couldn't take it out on him. The only people near us was a group of boys from our school. They were about fifteen rows below us. One of them was a kid that I could not stand. At school, he was always loud and abusive of others. He was taller than I and twice as wide. He was a farm boy, except he looked like he did farm work and lifted weights. To top it all off, he was extremely ugly. I had almost picked a fight with him at school when I had seen him throw a smaller boy out of a seat, but the bell had rung, and I had to get to class.

Now, here he was swearing at the refs and throwing pennies onto the floor. Something sparked in me, and I ran down and shoved him. He rolled down a few bleachers before catching himself. He jumped up with his fists raised and looked up at me. When he saw who his attacker was, he lowered them.

"Why'd you do that?" he whined.

"Because you are so ugly I need to beat your face in," I replied.

"No way. You just stay away from me you jerk. There is absolutely no way I'm going to fight you."

I saw his letterman's jacket on the seat where he had been and picked it up. I ran up the bleachers with it.

"Look," I yelled. "He puked all over, and I'm going to clean it up with this old rag."

"Give that back," he ordered while running toward me.

"You fight me, and I'll give it back."

"No," he screamed.

When I thought about what I was doing with his jacket, I got upset at myself. I had changed a bunch and hadn't realized it. I threw his jacket back, and he went to his seat.

This may have been the first time in the recent past that I had really analyzed my actions. I wondered why I had such hatred toward him. But I also hated that he was such a jerk. He always abused others and had a big mouth. Someone had to do him the favor of teaching him a lesson, and I decided it should be me. My hardcore hatred overshadowed my reasoning. I could see a need, a purpose that was out of my control. He had to be punished. Someone absolutely had to put him in his place. No one else was likely to do it, so it had to be my job. But I thought, *Doesn't that put me in the role of the bully? Was I being what I hated so much in others? Had the shadows turned their prey into a ravenous creature carrying out their dirty work? Was I now the one striking their targets for them?* I quickly assured myself that it wasn't so.

I sat and watched our team losing, and my anger erupted. I was being defeated and could not fight back. That team represented me. Pain and hurt, loneliness and fear of being weak, welled in my chest. My heart pounded loudly, and my mind signaled urgent messages of the need for action. I mustn't sit by and be abused. The noises around me were muffled echoes in a frenzied mind. I looked at my target. He was standing, swearing, throwing pennies at the refs. Rage flamed by my hurts, pains, fears, and vivid memories flashed before my darkened mind. *No, I wasn't a shadow. I was a target.* This loudmouth egomaniac was just another enemy attacking my private world. It was time for me to take the offensive. I could justify it because he was like the others who had picked on me. He was big, ugly, loud, and a bully. He was aggressive. All these call to arms he waved before me. It was time to fight—time to protect my small space, which he was intruding into.

I flew down the stands and shoved him hard from behind. I wanted him to react. A bigmouth like him would react before thinking so the surprise attack would get him to fight, I was sure.

He came up as quickly as he had gone down. He stopped one bleacher above me. There was no fear showing in his eyes, just darkness and hatred. The windows into his mind showed little dancing imps like I always saw in Dad. They were taunting and jeering at me.

For some odd reason, I began to regret my actions. His ugly pocked face could have scared most kids, but that wasn't what sparked my dilemma nor was it the thick broad shoulders and arms which were bigger than I had realized. I just felt wrong in what I was doing. I didn't go around looking for trouble, but I had assuredly started this.

He struck me in the mouth with a powerful fist. Immediately, I could taste the bitter saltiness of blood as it filled my mouth. Shreds of soft lip tissue lay limp on my tongue. There was a terrible ache in my teeth. They had sandwiched my lips between his broad fist. Water filled my eyes, and he became a fuzzy blur before me.

*I deserved that*, I thought. *I had acted like a jerk, so I deserved what I got.* I didn't fight back. Suddenly, another blow snapped my head and neck hard. Blackness stole my vision as bright sparkles flashed explosively through my head. The other side of my top lip swelled to match the first point of attack. More blood spurted into my mouth, and pain screamed through my face and neck. A dark shadow of weakness gripped me, and I wanted to lay down and rest. As my vision cleared a little, I could see the killer shadows dancing and yelling in his eyes. They wouldn't let him stop, not until I was seriously hurt. I knew that, but I also knew that I still deserved what he had given me. I started it, and I could take my punishment.

"You better fight back, or I'll get him," I heard my brother scream. "If you let him hit you again, I'm stepping in."

I looked to where he was standing. He was about thirty feet away and started toward us. No way would I let him get involved in this, not when I was at fault. While I was worrying over how to end this, the kid struck me again. This time, the pain sparked an eruption of anger. Banners of past abuses waved through my mind and began to scream for justice. I couldn't ignore it any longer. He had even hit me while I was looking away. My brother was at my side quickly, but he didn't need to be. I exploded into a fierce flurry of punches. Hatred swelled my veins with power to hit hard, fast, and accurately. I could feel his head bobbing back and to the sides as he tried to retreat and regroup. A hard solid right to the temple dropped him suddenly between the bleacher seats. I stood waiting for him to get to his feet. I was pleased with what I had done, but a sudden desire to finish a lesson which needed taught gripped me. It was difficult for me to refrain from jumping on him and pounding some more. I couldn't hit him while he was down though. He got slowly to his feet watching me carefully. His expression was totally new. The shadowy eyes were subdued and scornful. I didn't see or sense fear. He seemed to be studying, plotting a new attack. I waited for him to make a move, ready to resume my lesson.

Two of his friends came from behind and grabbed each of my arms. While they held on, he hit me for the fourth time in the mouth. Swelling had pressed my lips tight against my teeth and gums, and some of the shreds were cut loose completely. I felt no pain, just anger and desire to hit him more and more.

My brother kicked one of those holding my arms and sent him rolling down the stands. Someone else pulled the other away, and I took up where I had left off. I surged with energy. Blow after blow crunched on his face and head as I drove him backward and horizontally along the bleachers. I wasn't tired, wasn't breathing hard, and I was fixing this jerk thoroughly. I hoped he would stay standing for a long time. Another solid right dazed him. His arms dropped, eyes drooped, and his body sagged to the floor again. I quickly jumped on him. Sitting across his body and both arms to protect myself, I asked if he'd had enough. His face was pale and gaunt. His eyes showed no more fire and no more shadows. He looked very tired.

Again, two of his friends grabbed my arms and started pulling me off him. He yanked an arm free, reached up, and hit me in the mouth again. This time, the blow wasn't so hard, but it pinched my bottom lip on my teeth and released another screaming pain. Anger, hatred, and vengeance reared their ugly heads and drove me on. This guy was a cheap little coward, and this time, I would get even with the coward who was abusing me.

A boy from another school hit one of those holding my arms and sent him tumbling down the bleachers. A trail of blood from a gash over one eye marked his descent. My brother kicked the other boy in the face and began hitting him. I grabbed the jerk by the shirt with my left hand and slammed three vicious rights into his face. I was ready to hit him again when I looked into his eyes and saw nothing but milky white. His pupils were gone, and he had drooped deathly limp. A feeling of panic shot throughout my system. I was sure he was dead. I let go of his shirt, and he dropped to the floor. Scenes of prison flashed through my head. My stomach churned, and I almost vomited as I thought of living behind bars and, worst of all, what I had done to this kid.

Someone grabbed me from behind, lifting me off the corpse. I looked around and, for the first time, realized there was a large crowd around us.

"You'd better get out of here," the boy holding me warned. "The cops are coming."

"Come on," yelled my brother grabbing my arm.

There was a bathroom close by, and just as we were going into it, two cops came sprinting up the stairs past us.

I started to wash my face, and the water stung the raw flesh. Red liquid dripped freely through my fingers and streaked lines through the white basin, circling wildly; it dashed out of sight into darkness. The throbbing pain I had known before pulsated through my swollen mouth forcing pools of tears into my eyes. They marched defiantly through the gullies of my nose and cheeks and attacked the exposed flesh of my lips, stabbing spears of salt into my open wounds.

"Let's get out of here," my brother yelled.

We headed down the stairs. A girl from our school and her boyfriend ran up and sandwiched me between them.

"Come out with us," they warned. "Cops are all over the place looking for you."

"Man, I've never seen a fight like that," the boy observed.

"Yeah, I can't believe you let him hit you like you did," the girl added. "He wouldn't have even laid a hand on you if it weren't for his friends' interference. He deserved everything you gave him."

I didn't feel proud of my accomplishment even though they seemed to. I had done a dirty job that somehow had fallen to me. I was small, was skinny, and hated attention. The boy walking by me towered over me, and the girl was at least as tall as I was. I wondered why and how all these undesirable situations ensnared me. I also wondered why these people were so willing to help me. I didn't have friends. In fact, I had recently tried to pick a fight with the boy who was walking me out of this trouble.

I made it safely out of the building and hurried to my friend's car. He was already there along with my other brother.

My friend started yelling that he wanted to fight someone too. He could barely stand up in his drunken state, and we didn't need any more attention. My brothers and I loaded him up, and I drove us away.

On the way home, we passed one of our school busses. Kids started screaming and cheering when they saw us. I wasn't sure if it was about the fight, but I hoped it wasn't; I tried not to think about it. I just wanted to hurry home so I could get into bed and under my covers.

Back in Harden, I stopped at the local night spot to get some coffee for my friend. Before I got out of his car, someone ran up and told me to get out of town.

"The basketball coach heard what happened, and he asked the players to please beat the hell out of you," he informed me. "He also talked to some of the football kids. You better not be here when they show up."

That really riled me. *How could the coach possibly know what had happened? Why was I always judged so harshly? When kids picked on me, it was no big deal. Here, one time, I pick a fight, and now I am really a target. This time, anyone could be my attacker.*

When I got home, I tried to sneak quietly downstairs. I don't know why I felt the need for that because I was sure my parents couldn't know what had happened. Maybe it was just guilt.

"Is that you?" my parents asked calling my name.

"Yes, it's me," I answered.

"What happened tonight?" they asked.

"What do you mean?" I returned innocently.

"We have both felt that something bad had happened to you tonight. What was it?"

I gave them a quick abbreviated version of what had gone on and went to bed. I was sure the cops would show up any minute. I was engulfed in fear worrying that the kid was dead. I didn't tell my parents that though. I thought of how I hated this school, this town, and all the hypocritical jerks in it. They were as much responsible for what had happened that night as I was.

33

*But I am a worm, and no man;*
*a reproach of men, and despised of the people.*

—Psalms 22:6

The following day, I was very apprehensive about going to school. I knew I could fake sick and stay home, but I also knew I had to face it sooner or later. Sooner seemed to be better because if the boys at school thought I was afraid, they would be sure to attack. I would be walking into a den of lions, but I had to show no fear in order to keep them at bay. I wasn't sure I could do that. I was more terrified than at any other time in my life, and I never had felt so alone. My brothers offered to stay nearby. They could sense the seriousness of the situation also. I insisted they stay clear of the whole mess. No matter what happened they were not to get involved.

The reception I had imagined was not at all close to what I met. Almost everyone was glaring at me. I could see the dark shadows dancing in everyone's eyes. I could feel the hatred and bitterness I hadn't known before. This time, it was around me not within me. I began to fear for my life. My neck and back got tight and ached worrying that someone would hit me from behind or maybe even stab me. Groups of guys would move into my way in the hall, and I would curse and threaten them. They moved away slowly but only a seam wide enough for me to barely squeeze through. This brought strongly to my mind the verse in the Bible that talked about walking through the valley of the shadow of death. Only I did fear the evil I could sense crowding in around me. I doubted I would make it safely through the day. Things got worse as rumors spread. I heard that I had held the kid while one of my brothers beat him with a tire iron. This was even printed in the local paper. Another rumor told of me beating his head on a bus till he fell unconscious to the ground after which my brothers and I stomped and kicked him. Yet another said I was drunk and vomited on his coat after which I proceeded to beat his head on the concrete floor of the stands. Other newspapers throughout the valley reported different versions also. The only thing correct in any of them was my name, and that the kid was in the hospital with a concussion.

I did my best to stand tall as I could. I was afraid to show any fear. For someone who hated attention, I was in a real predicament. The longer the day went, the heavier I became. It was hard to stand up straight. I was tired, emotionally shredded. It seemed that everyone gained courage against me. Even the smaller boys, seeing everyone else cursing me, began to glare and threaten me. Many times I wanted to drop to my knees and cry from the loneliness and weakness that I felt. I was bewildered that such a small, insignificant person as myself could be such a center of attention.

Just after lunch, the principal sent a note to my class saying I was to leave the school grounds. The teacher read it out loud, and it brought a thunderous flash of cheering and snide jabs. My drunken friend had been kicked out earlier that morning. I was sure they had just let me stay half the day hoping I would get beat up.

Leaving the school grounds just reminded me of how unfair things were. Even though I had started the fight, the jerk had kept it going a lot longer than it should have gone. Absolutely no one cared about what really happened. I was glad the kid would survive, but I was upset enough that I would have hit him again if he were right there then. In fact, I was mad enough to fight any of the groups of boys who had threatened me that day.

A huge weight seemed to drift off my crushed body as I left the school. I felt I had won another victory, in a way. Having been there through the morning and lunch without any major incidents meant that I could probably survive this ordeal.

After school, my friend and I were driving around town. One of the biggest and meanest of the football players drove by. That he was there looking for me was no secret. He lived way out of town and close to the boy I had hurt. He always had farm chores, and I had never seen him just joyriding around town, something my friend and I did a lot.

When he saw us, he flipped us the bird. I was really miffed. I decided if I fought him and kicked the crap out of him, the rest of the school would leave me alone. We pulled up by him on my friend's side of the car. I leaned over where he could see me plainly.

"Do you want something?" I asked him tauntingly.

"Yes, I want to kick your butt," he sneered.

"That's fine with me," I shot back at him. "Let's go for it right now."

I grabbed the door and threw it open hard. All the tension, fear, and hatred of that day peaked right then. My arms and legs were shaking violently, and I couldn't speak as I approached his vehicle. No matter what happened, I was going to make sure he paid dearly for harassing me. Even more, I would make him pay for what that whole day had done to me. If I beat him up bad enough, it would scare at least most of the mobbers away.

"I'm not going to fight you," he yelled as he rolled up his window and locked his car door. "I'd like to kick the hell out of you though," he yelled through a small space where the window wasn't quite all the way up. "If I was sure I could, I would get out and do it. Besides, I'm not so sure now that things happened the way I heard them. You don't seem to be so cowardly as the coach told us you were."

His sudden change of tone set me back. *How could anyone care what really happened?* This was me, and I didn't matter.

"I'm willing to listen to your version before I make another judgment."

The sincerity in his statement calmed me enough that I could speak. I told him what had happened and admitted that I was the cause of the fight but not totally responsible for the end result. I even gave him names of those who had really watched the fight. He had heard one version from the hurt boy's friends, but it was a complete lie. This didn't surprise me, knowing that the wimp who got the MVP trophy for wrestling was one of his friends. That kid was a liar for sure.

The boy said he would check my story.

"What you say is so far from all I've heard," he said. "From your version, it was a fair fight. I promise I will let others know the truth if your story checks."

I was amazed but relieved. It was completely uncharacteristic for anyone to ask me what ever happened. I was just supposed to always be guilty.

When the boy found out the truth, he came back, shook my hand, and apologized. He said he knew the boy I beat up was a bigmouth a lot of the time. He even offered to help protect me. I thanked him but declined his offer.

"I don't want anyone else getting involved in this whole mess," I assured him.

The next morning, my father had to take me to school to get me reinstated. The principal told us coldly to go into his office. He had a major scowl on his face like all the kids around the school had. I guessed he was going to try to give us some verbal abuse. I knew my Dad wouldn't take that though.

"My son will stay out here, and you and I will go into your office to have the talk," Dad told him flatly. "I can settle this without him."

The principal turned red with embarrassment and anger. I thought I saw steam rising from his head. He was about six feet and an inch or two. My Dad was about five nine. Dad had a vicious temper though, and he had been a fighter when he was young. Since I almost never talked to him, I didn't know much of how he was, but uncles had told a few stories about him and his fights.

"You go sit down," Dad ordered the principal as he shut the door to the office. In less than five minutes, Dad walked out and told me I could go to class. The principal looked like a whipped puppy. He wouldn't even look at me. I wished I could have been in there. What a juicy story it would have made.

As days passed, the threats and glares subsided. The hurt kid spent a few days in the hospital and a couple at home before coming back to school. He was treated like a celebrity when he did return. The first time I saw him he had a big gauze bandage wrapped around his head. I was sure it was for show and to gain sympathy. I had an almost uncontrollable urge to go hit him in the mouth. I hated the sight of him.

# 34

*A pity beyond all telling*
*Is hid in the heart of love.*

—W. B. Yeats

My typing class was right after lunch. Type was one of my favorite classes. It was only offered for two years, but the teacher had arranged for me to take it a third year and still get credit for it. I was grateful and worked hard at it. I had my speed up to eighty-three words a minute with one mistake. That wasn't even close to the fastest typist, but it was good for me.

One day, I went to class early after lunch to catch up on some homework. We had assigned seats, which never changed. When I went into class, there was a girl there who sat directly behind me. She looked very occupied with what she was doing and didn't look up when I walked by. Just as I started to type, I felt a very light and gentle tap on my shoulder. I turned quickly to see what was needed. When I turned, the girl gasped and drew her hand away hurriedly. Her face was white with fear. I was worried that she might faint. That would really get me into big trouble. I wondered though if she was sick and needed me to go get help. She just sat there stiff and staring at me with her mouth partially open. It seemed that she wanted to speak but couldn't.

"Are you all right?" I asked her, concerned. This girl was one of the bunch of very modest, polite, and religious girls in our school.

She had short, dark-brown hair and a small, cute nose. Her face was rounded but with high cheek bones. She was quite attractive even without makeup, which I don't think she ever wore. I had been aware of her since my sophomore year when the kid I ran around with had pointed her and one of her friends out. He liked her friend, and I had been impressed with her at first sight. My buddy had told me who she was and how she wouldn't date until she was eighteen. I admired that. Now here she was alone with me in a room and had sought my attention. I realized now she was white because of who or what I was supposed to be. She nodded to my question about her being okay, but she seemed to be having trouble breathing.

"I...I...uh...I just wanted to tell you that I don't believe all the things people are saying about you," she stammered. "I don't think you are being treated fairly."

I could tell she was terrified. It had taken a lot of courage for her to tap my shoulder. She may not have believed whatever it was she had heard, but she was certainly afraid that it might be true or she wouldn't be so frightened. It gave me a boost though to know a girl like her would even talk to me. I didn't smoke or drink because I believed my body was something of a temple to be taken care of and kept clean, inside and out. Nonetheless, most kids in the school thought I was drunk more often than not. There were other stories about me much more vicious and some vulgar that I had heard but never paid any attention to.

"Thanks," I said as kindly as I could, hoping to help her relax. It was difficult for me to talk to her because I didn't think I was worthy to.

Slowly, a conversation developed, and by class time, she was smiling and telling me she knew I wasn't a bad person. Coming from her, that meant the world. It was great knowing that someone in the school didn't hate me and want to see me brutally harmed.

At the end of class, she tapped my shoulder again. This time harder and confidently. I looked at her, and her eyes were filled with tears. Some had escaped down her cheeks, while others dove onto her blouse in visible pools. My first thought was that she was crying because she felt ashamed for talking to an evil person like me.

"I am so sorry that I have gone to the same school with you all these years and never gotten to know you," she said very apologetically. "I just can't understand how such a decent person could be treated the way you have been. It is really unfair."

"Thanks very much," I replied trying hard to hold back my own tears. "You are very kind." I blushed.

There wasn't much school left, but for the rest of the year, we visited before class most days. Her sweet voice and happy face did much to disperse the black cloud that had built so thickly around me. It was warming and uplifting to have her talk so easily and freely with me. I greatly admired the courage it had taken for her to talk to me the first time.

Though she was a bright spot for me at that time, I still had many attackers. Frequently, someone would tell my brothers to let me know they were going to get me. Each time, I would find the person to oblige, and each time, they backed away. One who didn't though was my father. From the time he had gone to see the principal, he had turned very cold toward me. I was sure he hated me and resented me for it. When I had asked him what he told the principal, he said that it was none of my business, but that I for sure wouldn't have to worry about him bothering me again. All that had seemed to keep eating at him. He became very gruff with me at home. Whenever there was an argument between me and one of my brothers, he would threaten me through gritted teeth. With Dad, the gritted teeth meant he was ready to strike.

One Saturday morning, we were all watching TV. I was sitting in a lounge chair, and my older brother came over and told me to get out so he could sit there. I refused, so he sat on my lap. I pushed him off just as Dad walked into the room.

"What the hell is going on?" he boomed.

"I was sitting here, and he came and told me to get out so he could sit here," I defended myself.

"Well, both of you get out, and I'll sit there," he ordered. "I don't want to hear another word from either of you."

I could tell he was in a real bad mood. I moved over to the couch and sat down. I was the only one on the entire couch. My brother followed me over and sat on my lap again. His bony rear hurt my leg as he twisted around to make himself heavier.

"Knock it off, and leave me alone, you stinkin' jerk," I yelled at him.

Dad looked at us and demanded what was going on.

"He followed me over here and sat on my leg," I complained. I shoved him off and scooted away.

"Just stay away from me," I blared.

Dad jumped up quickly. Before I knew what was going on, he had hit me on the left side of my face with his doubled up fist. The blow knocked me over the arm of the couch and onto the floor. As he had come toward me, my brother had moved away as if he knew what was going to happen. I immediately wondered if they had set the whole thing up. Whatever it was, from that time on, my hatred toward Dad was intensified greatly. Even though I had feared and hated him and things he did before that, I had still respected him as my father. Now I didn't respect him at all. I didn't even like him. He was no different than any other of my enemies in that cold, hard town. The dark shadows danced around and laughed at me through his eyes. It seemed that he had thoroughly enjoyed hitting me.

To add to the bleakness of graduation time, a group of students and teachers had gotten together to petition the school not to allow me to graduate. I was a disgrace to them and the community and therefore should not be included among them.

I didn't know anything of this movement until it was over. I was told that they had gone into a faculty meeting where the group of students and teachers were aggressively pursuing their

204 | KEN LILJENQUIST

goal and that it had all ended when the type teacher had stood up for me and really given them heck.

During the practices for graduation, we had to sit in alphabetical order. That placed me between two more of the nice, religious girls. For the first two days, they both sat still in their chairs with their eyes frozen forward. They always looked pale or angry or both. It upset me that they would be forced to sit by me. Here they were at an event of their lives, which was so important to them, and they couldn't enjoy it because they had to sit by…whatever they thought I was. I became sick worrying over it. It was unfair to them. I didn't really care at all about the whole show, and I considered butting out of it. On the third day of practice, they looked so miserable that I almost started crying. Pity and sorrow flooded my mind and heart so fully that I had a tough time fighting back the tears. I decided I would be sick from then on and not show up. Shortly after my decision, one of the girls dropped a paper she had been holding. I instinctively bent down and picked it up for her. As I turned to hand it to her, we almost bumped heads. She had bent to get it too.

"Oops, I'm sorry," I said, staring right into her watery eyes. I wondered if these two spent nights crying about this. I could imagine them and their friends discussing the terrible injustice they were being subjected to. Now seeing the watered up soft eyes of such a decent girl dropped me to the depths of shame. I actually wanted to hug her and tell her not to cry because I would be sick for graduation, so she would have to sit by me.

Some sort of light spread quickly across her face bringing back its color. The water in her eyes began to sparkle, and a broad smile stretched across her face.

"Oh, thank you," she said cheerfully. "You're quite a gentleman."

"Not many people think that," I countered. "I'm not very well liked around here."

"Maybe everyone is like me. Maybe they had heard and judged you incorrectly. I thought you were a mean, vicious person. I've been afraid if I made one wrong move, you'd hit me."

"I'd never do that," I said. "I'd never hit a girl. I'd probably want to stomp anyone who did. You know, I don't even like fighting, but too many kids won't leave me alone."

"Wow, this is so neat," she beamed. "I can't wait to tell my friends. They'll never believe it." She was acting as though she had just met some very important person or something. During our next break, she ran over to a group of girls and was talking excitedly and pointing in my direction.

Through the rest of the practices, I talked freely with both the girls. Actually, they did most of the talking. I was still very shy around girls. If I hadn't had such deep feelings of sorrow for these two, I probably wouldn't have been able to be sociable. Practices became great for us all, and they both expressed regret at not getting to know me over the years we had been in school.

Graduation night was exhilarating. The two girls by me both cried and hugged me, which scared me, but I was grateful. The girl from type class cried the worst. She was a senior too and was handing a flower to each person as they walked past with their diplomas. When I got close to her, she burst into tears, stepped forward, and gave me a very affectionate hug.

"I am so sorry," she said calling me by name. "I'll always regret not getting to know you better. I feel very ashamed."

Wow, attention, and good attention from three different people at the same time. I wasn't sure how to react. I thought I would burst with happiness. The few kids I had as friends in school weren't really friends. I hung around some once in a while, then some others once in a while, but there weren't any real attachments. But the three girls were sincere. It radiated from them. I knew they were sincere. Such treatment was alien to me. They really liked me just the way I was. I was sure they were aware of my fighting but still they accepted me. No graduation present could have been better than this. When I walked away from the girl from type class, tears flowed down my cheeks, and I didn't even feel embarrassed by it. I just imagined what all the past years could have been like if I had made some real friends. A dark shadow then clouded my mind. My targeting must have been deliberate. What did it all mean? Perhaps now my dark enemy had let loose just enough to show me what I had missed. Perhaps this was just another shrewd attack from a different angle to lift me up and then drop me down again. It didn't matter though. Those last few minutes and those girls' warmth was a cherished blessing.

I went home and cried myself to sleep that evening. I couldn't tell if it was happiness, pain, or a mixture of the two.

On Saturday morning, I was up watching television. Dad walked into the room and told me to go outside and do some yard work. I got up and walked to the door. Just as I touched the knob to open the door, I was jerked around by Dad, and he doubled his fist and knocked me to the floor.

"You think you're a real tough man, don't you?" he asked arrogantly.

Looking up into his eyes, I could see those cruel and laughing imps dancing around. Behind them was total darkness. There wasn't even a glimmer of love or caring. *What could possibly bring this on?* I was destitute of any reason for this hatred toward me. I wanted to ask Mom why and get some sparkle of hope for justification for his disdain for me. I could hear in my mind the pat answer Mom would give.

"Oh, he doesn't mean anything by it. Just ignore it," she would say.

I realized how right Mom was. There are some things in life that can't be rectified or understood. Maybe that was my major trial in life. I was so emotionally irrational, so I needed to learn to just ignore it.

## 35

*Whomever the raven rends attains salvation.*

—Halldór Laxness

So here I sit on the slope of this high mountain. The warm rays of the sun are comforting. I feel calm and peaceful as I watch an eagle glide freely above the high mountains. Silently, a shadow creeps from behind me and cuts off the warmth of the sun's glow. The small breeze barely noticeable before caresses my arms raising hundreds of cold chills along my bare skin. Pulling my knees to my chest, I fold my arms over them and rest my chin on the back of one hand. Warm pools form in the corners of my eyes. They dart and land coldly on my cheeks and run a chilling path to my chin. There, they hang briefly quivering in the breeze then cut loose and lay lifeless on my arms. More pools form and two steady streams follow. My heart freezes deep within my weary soul. My surroundings darken as a plea for help screames forth.

"Where do I belong?"

Then I wonder, *maybe it isn't me. Maybe I just need to get out of this stinkin' place.*

A passage of scripture floods my mind:

> For the mountains shall depart, and the hills be removed; but my kindness shall not depart from thee, neither shall the covenant of my peace be removed, saith the Lord that hath mercy on thee.
>
> Isaiah 54:10